A Man of Worth

By Simon A Cohen

An Inspector Reynolds Murder Mystery

First published 2026 by B340 Press, Alexandra, Vic

ISBN: 978-1-7645293-0-3

Also available in kindle edition: **ISBN:** 978-1-7645293-2-7

1 2 3 4 5 6 7 8 9 10

To Andrea

—   something to read on your birthday.

I went down to the Infirmary,
Saw my baby there,
Stretched out on a long white table,
So cold, so sweet, so fair.

Don Redman and Joe Primrose

The station's public address crackled into life; the voice was strong, practised.

"The train now standing on platform 1 is the 8:30 to Albury, stopping at Seymour, Benalla and Wangaratta."

The announcement was made without emotion, why should it be anything more, it was nothing the guard hadn't said a hundred times before, except for the current additional reminder.

"Passengers are advised, due to current Covid-19 health regulations, facemasks are required to be worn at all times on this service."

Early morning autumn sunshine slanted through the train window illuminating the tired upholstery. In a nation of car enthusiasts, the regional railway is an unfashionable way to travel and received little by way of public funding. Most of those on the platform were students, elderly or in some way, judging by their wardrobe, socially disadvantaged. There was no designer luggage on display, no haute couture, beyond the counterfeits that had been purchased in Bali before overseas flights had been paused. The would-be passengers hurried down the platform selecting which carriage to board, some trying hard to maintain their practical and safe social distancing, others pushing and shoving to get the best seats. Tom was one of those who stood well back, a tall, slender, middle-aged man; slightly grey and slightly shabby. If he looked in part like an eccentric science teacher, well, there was a good reason for that. Tom displayed the same dishevelled air often seen in single men in their forties, those who in their youth had upheld the highest of dress standards but whose aging attire confirmed they had not been shopping for a decade, and certainly never in the company of their wife. His jacket was strategically patched, his shoes a weary unbrushed suede; he wore a pork pie hat high on the back of his head, half a size too small.

As the train pulled out from Melbourne the chattering of the carriages was matched by the wheezing strains of the air-conditioner fighting valiantly against the day's steadily rising temperature. Soon it would be uncomfortably hot; not the dry blistering heat of an Australian summer, luckily that extreme was already over for another year, but for the passengers behind their assorted face-masks it would still be a grim heat, and difficult to tolerate.

The front carriage required passengers to walk a little further from the ticket turnstile, making it normally the easiest one in which to find a good seat. Today it was nearly empty and Tom had no trouble locating two adjacent vacant seats. Discovering two not covered in chip papers and plastic drinks bottles was somewhat harder; wasn't there supposed to be additional cleaning these days, extra precautions being taken? Tom made the mistake of sitting at a table, one side in a grouping of four seats, in the hope the seats opposite would remain empty. Sitting at a table was always a risk in that way, there was always the chance it would lead to an unwelcome brief encounter, but at least he could look out the window and see where he was going without the disconcerting and unnatural feeling of travelling backwards.

Accompanying Tom on the train was a small overnight bag and a large double-bass. The disparity in size between the two illustrated Tom's priorities, as did the fact he had bought an extra ticket so his prized instrument could sit next to him. The alternative was unacceptable, the bouncing over the points was bad enough for bass as it was and he was not going to abandon it completely in the luggage compartment to languish forlornly with the more mundane items of baggage.

Railways were not Tom's favourite mode of transport but, having lost his driving licence earlier in the year, Tom had been forced to rediscover the joys and peculiarities of Victoria's public transport system. Knowing it was in a way his own fault did nothing to assuage his resentment of the delays it caused to his current travel arrangements; Tom considered a little speeding as a minor offence, something everyone did at some point. Shouldn't a punishment be proportional to the offence; after all who had his speeding even hurt? Was it truly justice when the inconvenience caused by his driving ban so far outweighed any time which he may have saved by his driving too fast in the first place? If he, as a teacher, had tried to impose six months of detentions on a pupil for being five minutes late, well he'd hate to think what would happen, yet criminal justice and natural justice were not equivalent, apparently, and his occasional attempt to be five minutes early had been met harshly.

The trip from Melbourne Southern Cross to Wangaratta was not scheduled to be a long one, according to his timetable it would only take about three hours. When he had travelled the route previously those prior journeys had inevitably been met with replacement coach services and persistent delays which had left Tom desperately looking at his watch in a futile attempt that this action would somehow effect an increase in the trains speed. Tom was optimistic today's trip would be swifter and he would make good time, even so three hours onboard a hot stuffy train could feel like three days, as could three hours spent wearing a face-mask, anywhere. He wondered what would happen if he removed his mask; would anyone even notice, could the guard fine him for removing it, would the other passengers remove theirs too in a spontaneous display of solidarity, or perhaps they would report him for breaking one of the state's few onerous Covid restrictions. He was pretty sure face masks were still a requirement, and if not they were certainly a good idea anyway. For all the inconvenience it remained a speculation he decided not to put to the test.

Coming to think of it. Tom was unsure what the current round of Covid restrictions were. Travel bans had been lifted, and he was sure face masks were no longer generally being worn indoors, although it was still necessary to sign a contact register for shops and cafes, he had even gone to the trouble of installing a QR code app on his phone to make that procedure less onerous. Also, where bars and cafés were concerned, while not back to normal, they had been allowed to reopen and operate under some customer restrictions. One customer per four square metres came to mind, or was it one per two square metres. Tom was unclear, the rules had changed so often from lock-down to lock-down it was hard to follow. Certainly, there was some statutory social distancing in the hospitality industry, which he supposed those in charge were following closer than he was, and hopefully implementing.. Tom wondered how many people would therefore be allowed tonight at his gig, probably considerably more than would turn up anyway. His experience of pub jazz gigs was that packing in too large audience was never a problem. Anyway, while he had played large venues, and big festivals, over the years this trip was more about catching up with old friends who he'd not seen since the start of the whole Covid-19 outbreak. He'd be happy jamming with friends and any audience at all would be, in Tom's mind, a bonus.

The real trouble about trains was Tom had never bought into the false glamour which occasionally surrounded rail travel; the allure of 1920's steam-and-cocktail parties. Melbourne Southern Cross to Wangaratta was a far cry from the Orient Express, and he was no Belgium detective. In short, he could only amuse himself for so long by looking out the window at the hurtling countryside whilst playing a solitary game of eye spy. It didn't take long before one field looked identical to the next, a rural expanse of indistinguishable agricultural similarity. In simple terms, Tom got bored on trains and try as he did to dispel the cloud of his disinterest through reading books and drinking peppermint tea, neither seemed to work successfully for long, although the tea did give him an effective excuse to periodically lower his mask and breathe in the increasingly stale air. He even tried to amuse himself by sending text messages to his friends, but the brief intervals this relief allowed him, were themselves, limited by the spasmodic nature of rural phone reception. He knew that at some point in the trip he would be reduced to opening his double bass' case and humming the sheet music.

Across from Tom, on the other side of the table, a mousey middle-aged lady came and sat down. She was small, seeming smaller still by the way she sat hunched over some knitting, with long dull hair draped in amongst her balls of wool. Her pale colouring and pastel dress contrasting the brightly patterned cardigan she was engaged in producing. On her face-mask she had painted a broad unmoving grin giving her the overall appearance of a psychotic marionette. Before the train had even left the station, she began clicking away at her knitting in a perfect four/four time; knit, knit, knit, knit / knit, knit, knit, purl. Behind his face-mask Tom couldn't help himself smiling; a big four even Buddy Bolden would have been happy to work with.

They had hardly left the outskirts of Melbourne, and with the last of its impersonal ever-expanding new suburbs still in view, when the mousey woman decided to strike up a conversation. She looked at Tom's instrument case, covered in stickers stating things like "Keep Music Live", "Handel with Care" and "Jazz by the Bay – Artist Access," and so, prompted by these, she chose to start with the somewhat obvious, "do you play?" An opening line as decaffeinated as Tom's beverage.

Tom found himself being uncharacteristically rude.

"Not on the train."

Tom knew it had been the wrong thing to say almost at once. He was not habitually a rude person, and just because he was unhappy about having to take yet another tiresome rail trip, was that actually a good enough reason to take his frustration out on this woman? Regretting his petulant display of bad manners, he added, "do you?" part as an afterthought and part as an apology.

"Oh no, well not any more. Not since I had children."

Tom was a bachelor, and although he had dated women who were mothers, this proved something of a puzzling answer for him, his scant personal experience being insufficient to enable him to rapidly equate the presence of children in your home to the limitations they could impose on your available practice schedule. For Tom, as a teacher, children disappeared promptly at 3:30 on weekdays, and were never seen at weekends if they could be avoided. Still, he managed to say something like, "you should, maybe you could play with your kids."

His voice was quiet yet clear and as he spoke Tom tapped his finger on the table in an undemonstrative drumming way, a subconscious mannerism he had acquired over the years. When he listened, he generally found something to fidget with, although all the time maintaining eye contact with a thoughtful precision as if the knitting woman's opinions were of the highest importance to him, they weren't, but he was a good listener.

It was a largely unwanted conversation only passing the time somewhat better than his dull book; Tom regularly made the mistake of buying high-brow books he liked the thought of reading rather than the sort he actually enjoyed reading in practice. On this trip Tom was being accompanied by a particularly worthy volume, a book which he was finding unreadably dull.

By the time she left the train at Seymour station Tom knew as much about her as he could ever have wanted to. She had told him she was travelling to meet her brother who was stationed at the nearby Puckapunyal army base. She had discussed her children and the difficulties of home schooling. She had described her last holiday, to the Gold Coast, illustrating these recollections with pictures from her phone. She even told him what films she liked watching, almost all of which contained a number in the title and were, it seemed, even better than near identical films of lesser numbers. Finally, because Tom was such an interested listener, she had shared information about both of her unsuccessful marriages in details that would have made almost any analyst blush. At one point in the conversation, she mentioned because of her job as a dental technician she could get him cut price dental care, an assumption about the value she attached to what she called "a perfect smile" which he found slightly offensive in several ways, particularly as the current state of his teeth was unknown to her, hidden as it was behind his Covid face-mask. What was perfect about one type of smile anyway? Before leaving, she had given him her phone number, unasked for. She was not really his type, not her fault, but there it was, apart from anything else he made it a rule not to date random people he had only just met on public transport, or as Tom succinctly put it, "nutters on trains." Of course, if there was yet another lockdown, he may be forced to make that more of a guideline than an actual rule. Dating opportunities had been near impossible for weeks and were only now slowly starting to open again as venue restrictions were beginning to lift. Tom duly pretended to enter her details into his phone's contact book so as not to upset her. Instead, he had in fact been checking the time, nearly ten o'clock, half way. Only, an hour and a half of peace and quiet to go and he should be arriving at Wangaratta. Just Tom, alone again with his beloved and much valued bass; an instrument which like all things of real value he had given a name, Genevieve.

The bass itself, from an instrument dealer's point of view, was not a particularly significant one. Genevieve hadn't, for example, been made by the hand of a famous 18th century luthier. What she did display however was a particularly high standard of relatively contemporary craftmanship, a finish giving her both good tonal range and, significantly to Tom, a considerable degree of jazz oomph. Important characteristics which belied Genevieve's relatively modest and recent pedigree. Even so, she had cost Tom significantly more money than in truth he could honestly afford on his teaching salary. Whenever he was asked about her price, all he would say, displaying his normal degree of tasteful discretion, was she, had cost him, "enough," all the while displaying a degree of care towards her which suggested, "enough" was actually, "a lot," but as Tom had also once said, "what price can you put on beauty?" A remark which for Tom had nothing to do with the state of a person's teeth. Genevieve's cost and worth were two distinct concepts, and whatever Genevieve's price amounted to, it was certainly one which Tom, given his current priorities, had been readily prepared to pay.

The track from Seymour to Wangaratta ran through an unremarkable stretch of countryside; the north eastern part of Victoria had obviously seen little rain recently. Field after field of dead khaki-coloured tussocks flashed past, the colour of sun-dried soil and rural misery, the colour being as if mother nature had found a way of providing a constant reminder of the stress which she was being caused by the ever-rising annual heat; a temperature slowly being matched inside the carriage since the ailing air-conditioner had exhaled its last cooling puff and finally died.

Tom started looking at his watch every few minutes.

A fly landed on him and was quickly brushed aside; not long now.

A baby further down the carriage began to cry; not long now.

One of the carriages wheels started to squeak alarmingly; hopefully, not long now.

Finally, the train was slowing, houses once again coming into view; a football oval, some warehouses, more houses, a pub, a signal box, the station platform. They had arrived; more or less on time all along.

As Tom opened the train-door he was hit by the midday heat outside, for all its apparent inadequacy the trains air-conditioner had maintained some small degree of internal cooling, still, it was good to finally take his mask off.

He was met on the platform by old friends, a couple. The man grabbed Tom's small overnight bag and swung it over his shoulder, and in return gave him a, " 'right mate," as a greeting. The woman gave him a hello kiss.

It was good to see them again, people he felt so comfortable with, and who he didn't have to make small-talk to when he didn't feel in the mood. People who weren't about to ask him inconsequential stuff about movies or holiday destinations. Friends with whom he shared his passion for important, valuable things, created with artistry, like music.

As they walked out towards the carpark together, they were in perfect step.

The auger's motor rattled as it idled; its drilling tool rotating slowly even without the motor being correctly engaged: the machine was having a tough day. In hindsight, Pete King knew he should have used his tractor's post hole digger today, but he had not anticipated how baked dry and heavily compacted the soil would be, how little moisture would be left in it even this close to the creek. Pete was as stubborn as any farmer could be, if he had to struggle on such a hot day so could his tools. He would try and get the job finished by tea, if not his temporary fix of an electric wire should be good for another night. He hadn't lost any cows yet and had no intention to start today.

It was tough work in the midday heat and the aging farmer would have benefited from some help; fencing was a young man's job anyway. Unfortunately, he was having to work alone these days, farmhands worth their wages were few and far between. Recently he had let a young lad go, his certificate in agricultural science proving not to be worth the paper it was printed on; a wizard with a computerised stock pedigree app maybe, but little practical skill, and his five days a week and nine to five work ethic had made the lad incompatible with farm life. Young people seemed to demand a better work-life balance than in his day, not that Pete could blame them; he had always counted himself one of the lucky ones marrying Joanne all those years ago.

From his vantage point Pete had a good view up the hill to the farm's main house, it was not where he lived; he did not own the land he worked, he was an employee. It was not that he didn't like his job, or that he was poorly paid for performing it, rather his lack of proprietorship doing nothing to help ease his aching muscles at the end of the day.

As he worked the cattle stood around watching him, their long eyelashes flashing in the hope he was going to somehow produce a bale of hay. They needed no supplementing, they were in good condition, well fed and ready to fetch a good price. He was proud of the herd he had built up over the last few seasons; solid animals with four sturdy corners, Herefords. Sometime Pete found himself wondering if he would be prouder if they really were his own cows instead of animals he merely managed, but he didn't dwell on it for long; he was a farmer, rooted in the day-to-day reality of life on the land, he couldn't afford to expend his energy in futile day dreams.

Pete positioned the last pole in its newly drilled hole; cheap treated pine, but it would see him out, and it was not his farm anyway. It was time to begin the wiring, time to turn the neat row of wooden posts into a fence. Before starting, he would have a drink, a swig of water from his bottle; he had earned it.

Unlike many older farmers Pete King was safety conscious. He wore shatter-proof glasses and ear plugs, small precautions, some protection from minor incidents, even if they offered him reno real defence should a wire fail under tension. Given the still idling auger and the dulling effect of his ear plugs Pete hardly heard the noise. Not loud enough to be sure what it was anyway. Pop, pop, possibly thought Pete, a gun, nothing to be alarmed about. The sound of guns wasn't uncommon in the countryside, and he often took the odd feral deer himself when they strayed onto the farm. The double pop suggested a shot gun. He looked around for the shooter. Surely it wouldn't be Donald today, not on a Tuesday, and what would he be after at this time? It was too late in the day for rabbits, and too early in the year for ducks. He looked down at his watch, 1:59pm.

Turning back up the hill to face the big house he saw a white van departing. So, he thought, the noise had only been a van back-firing. Time to go back to work if he was ever going to get the fence finished. Putting his water bottle down, and turning the auger completely off, he returned to his fencing unaware of the significance to his life of the sound he had just heard.

The students had spent the morning engaged in the surreal pursuit of moving a mannequin dressed in pyjamas from one hospital bed to another. It was part of their training and, surrounded by others performing the same pointless task, they saw nothing odd in it; all part of becoming a nurse.

The course had been badly affected by pandemic lockdowns. Most of the lectures had been changed to on-line learning, but even this hadn't prevented all of the now numerous delays. If they had kept to the original schedule the cohort would already be qualified, but as it was, they faced another six months before they would finally see a diploma in their hands. For many of them it was all taking too long, and some had even been forced reluctantly to drop out.

When not studying, they had come from various walks of life; a few straight from school, but most, slightly older, were seeking a new vocation. If there was a common link between them it was none had come from well-paid professions, their new one would not be either; nursing had never been a pathway to financial riches, its rewards coming in other ways. The current group of students' disparate backgrounds included; shop assistants, hairdressers, waitresses, and one had even been a tour guide. That was before Covid had hit the globe and a younger generation had seen their casualised employment disproportionately badly hit. Between them, the students, had lost months of work in the successive lockdowns and only now were starting to get some shifts back; normality trying hard to return under the cloud of yet another outbreak, another lockdown. The Government's special Covid-19 Job-keeper payments had helped of course, even if they had the feeling the scheme had helped their bosses considerably more than it had helped them; middle class welfare to cushion the pandemic blow to the administration's voter base. For the young students the effects were still being felt; credit cards had reached their limits, rent remained in arrears, current accounts had been cleaned out, and those little tins on the mantlepiece for holiday savings had long since been emptied and spent on groceries. It helped that the training course was free, a government policy designed to address all the unfilled jobs in health care. There were plentiful advertised vacancies waiting for them when they qualified. They hoped their depleted finances could hold out that long. If not, well that was something they really didn't want to think about.

And so, as they practiced the correct technique for moving a plastic body around a simulated hospital ward, in case they were ever placed in the position of having to administer nursing care to a synthetic patient, many of their minds wandered; should they get new shoes for their sore feet, were their false nails really that much of an infection risk, why couldn't they wear a real nursing uniform instead of these shapeless theatre scrubs. Maybe, they discussed among themselves, they could get a shift or two doing vaccinations, surely you don't need to be fully qualified to stick a syringe into someone's arm. Some were even engaged thinking that at least their disrupted training was for a new career where their future employment would not rely on the current level of Covid restrictions, and how their pay from now on would therefore be unaffected by any lockdowns.

One student in particular was at the stage of mentally planning how long it would take to repair her exhausted savings, when, unknown to her, and without doing anything herself, she experienced a significant increase in her wealth. It was not an economic windfall she would know about for several days, and when she eventually found out, it would be from a completely unexpected source.

Lunchtime at the Railway Café was always busy. They had somehow even managed to maintain a steady trade in the last lockdown by providing an additional evening take away service. It was true, some of the table staff had seen a reduction in their hours, but the proprietors had done their best to ration out the available work so as to keep everyone they could employed. A couple of the waitresses had, on their own initiative, even run a home delivery service that had proved popular. Still, it was good to be able to open up again, even with the two square meter per customer rule leading to a slight reduction in the restaurant's seated capacity.

Today saw a fairly typical lunchtime service. The restaurant was well patronized, the door wedged open and the ceiling fan rotated slowly to maintain a languid flow of air around the busy tables. The waitress recognised a number of regulars who today included; some TAFE students discussing their morning tutorial, a pair of senior doctors from the hospital comparing their uncomplimentary notes about a young registrar, and a small group from the council office up the street who always came in at least once a week. It was that sort of restaurant, the type which encouraged a regular clientele by its friendly service and niche menu offering a whiff of the unconventional by containing several vegetarian and vegan options and plenty of specialty spiced central American dishes. The staff addressed many of the customers by name, some of whom had regular orders; there was a good atmosphere.

Seated at table 4, by himself, a businessman gobbled down his solo lunch, nachos. He sweated slightly from the jalapeño chillies and took large gulps from the table water as he ate. Between mouthfuls he was having a noisy argument on his phone. He was not so selfish as to do so on speakerphone but try as they did to enjoy their own meals in peace the other customers couldn't help themselves overhearing his tirade, and listening to his swearing was doing little to enhance their digestion. The disturbance, in the small space, was such that, after a several minutes of listening to his abusive outbursts, many of the other customers had made comments. Eventually the waitress had gone over and spoken to him. She had not wanted to, she knew him as one of her regulars, and one accustomed to leaving a healthy tip.

The businessman seethed in response, settled his account, without his customary additional gratuity, and stormed out the door. Had the waitress known the man had been partaking of his final meal and within the hour he would be dead, she may have been even less willing to intervene. As it was, she disinfected his seat and re-set the table for the next customer.

Under most circumstances qualified chartered accountants, by the very nature of their profession, know their own worth and insist on receiving it, paid in full on a monthly basis. But as every rule is proved by its exceptions, and Sally Kendall was, in terms of her financial payments, that rules confirming omission. Not for profit industries are well known for their comparatively poor pay, and Sally, as the registrar and finance manager for the Anglican Diocese of Wangaratta, receive something less than her professions normal salary. However, Sally happily did so, basking in the sure and certain knowledge that her sacrifice was for a good cause, the Lords good no less.

Today that certainty was being somewhat eroded. For the past six hours she had been in a meeting with the acting administrator of the diocesan aged care facility concerning the residential home's ongoing registration documentation. It was dull work indeed and the whole nursing home seemed to be run at a year-round 27 degrees Celsius, making conditions in the meeting room close to intolerable, even when they were joined at midday by the Bishop of Wangaratta, who always brought with him an eccentric sense of humour considerably more delicious than the uninspired dried out egg and cheese sandwiches provided as a simple lunch.

Also attending today's marathon meeting were the nursing home's acting unit manager, acting operations officer, the

CEO of Blue Homes and for most of the morning at least a local solicitor. The registration meeting was purportedly the final stage of the nursing facilities' take over by the Blue Homes Group, a process that was supposed to be a formality. Why, wondered Sally, was it that whenever a solicitor turned up things started to get more complicated; it had been that way in her divorce and it was happening again now. She was grateful that he was working pro bono, but really, hadn't all this legal stuff been sorted out in principle twelve months ago? Frankly she was glad when he left at lunchtime, after all the sale had already been finalised and the necessary registrations transferred, his invitation at this belated stage had been a courtesy one anyway.. If there really was a form they had missed in the complex conveyancing process, how did it require six hours to fill it in? It was a feeling not helped by Sally still being in two minds about disposing of yet another of the Church's assets. Wasn't it part of their core function, she wondered, to care for the poor, the sick and the elderly? It may make administrative sense to outsource some specialised services in these days of excessive and complex regulation, but where do you draw the line, Holy Communion?

By four in the afternoon the meeting was finishing up much to the relief of all the participants. They had spent the best part of the day closeted together in the stuffy room, face masks hung around their necks, phones on mute and cut off from the rest of the world; when they emerged, they would discover the events which had transpired in their absence.

Chapter 1 - Tuesday Evening

She wants somebody, who's workin' all day
So she's got money, when she wants to play

Percy Venable

There was an acrid smell in the room even with the small window thrown wide open in a futile attempt to combat the pungent mix of spilt beer and stale take away food. Still, they had been in plenty of worse greenrooms over the years waiting for their gig to start and there was no reason to be surprised by the state of this one behind a small country pub.

A head appeared at the door. "Whenever you're ready."

The three of them hadn't done any shows together for a while, not since Covid had caused all the live music venues to be closed down last year, so there were a few more nerves in the room than normal.

"Right" said Tom, "let's get this show on the road."

Tom was first on stage, carefully positioning himself on the left-hand edge of the small platform as unobtrusively as his double-bass would allow. Even after all these years of performing he was still something of a self-conscious artist and until the musical muse took him over, he all but hid behind Genevieve. A friend had once joked if he could have played from behind a screen then he probably would have. The joke was not far from its mark.

June came next, floating onstage wearing what would have once, in a more gracious age, been described as a cocktail frock. The pub's multi-coloured stage lighting paying scant justice to her flowing strawberry blond waves, and striking good looks, an appearance not in any way spoilt by her ethnic jewellery and air-cushioned boots.

In most bands the singer is the last one onstage but June had always been superstitious about being left behind, an uncharacteristic trait for someone whose day job and credentials as a doctor marked her as a well-educated woman. It was even more peculiar when you considered it was her name which topped on the handbill, *The June White Trio;* the name being an anomaly left over from when she had played clarinet. These days June's dusky voice was her only instrument.

That only left Clark the pianist, or tonight given the logistics of carrying his piano around regional Victoria, the keyboardist. Forty something, good looking, serious.

They played *Stardust,* and the room swayed. Clark's hands shuffled over the keys, glancing and tapping, hovering, occasionally holding one long enough to sound a full rich note, and then drifting off again into Hoagy Carmichael's dream. June's voice added an occasional mellow accent but always leaving plenty of room for Clark's piano to drift in and out, and all the while Tom kept a tight grip onto the tune's rhythms like holding a fish's tail as it splashed just under the surface of an icy pond. If you closed your eyes, it was the 1920's and you couldn't even see the TV above the bar showing a repeat of last night's footy game. If you used your imagination hard enough you could hardly hear the electronic blip, blip, blip of the slot machine in the corner.

It was a good gig, there were almost forty people there, and maybe half were even listening. Getting twenty jazz fans to a pub gig in rural Victoria on a hot Tuesday evening, not bad at all, even this close to Wangaratta where the punters are a bit more knowledgeable about jazz than in most places. Another gig or two like this and they'd be ready for the festival at the end of the month, maybe. That's assuming it was still going ahead, which given all the Covid-19 upheaval was a sizable assumption.

They played for around forty-five minutes before finishing with *Honeysuckle Rose,* one of June's favourites. Perhaps next time they would play something else at the end of the set. Maybe some Cole Porter, a little easier for the audience to hum on the way home after the show. Not everybody was going home tonight, Tom was sleeping on Clark's couch before heading back to Melbourne early tomorrow. Occasionally June did a gig with Clark as her accompanist but it worked better when all three of them could play together. Sometimes other friends would join in with their improvised musical conversation for the odd number, there were no rules, it was Jazz, whoever turned up played. To get Tom onto the train for tonight's show, they had encouraged his attendance with the offer of one of Clark's big breakfasts the next day. Not that Clark was a good cook, but anyone can make a passable bacon and eggs. Tonight, the pub was feeding them, a big Parma and chips with enough beer on the rider to float a battleship if required. A few years ago, it may have been, but these days, well, everyone slows down at some point, don't they?

Back in the green room they all simultaneously exhaled as if they had been holding in their last breath since starting their performance; onstage could be as asphyxiating as it was exhilarating. There was a group hug, rather awkwardly between Tom and Clark, a mixture of relief and satisfaction knowing they had done well, yet experienced enough to, at the same time, know what they had to work on for next time; overall a good outing. There was so much adrenaline they could probably have done it all over again if June's voice could hold out long enough. Maybe just one more number, an encore. They could do a Cole Porter song after all, yes, *Let's do it, let's fall in love.*

Clark checked his phone. He couldn't have said why, just a habit probably. There had been three missed calls, all from the station. He knew it was about to ruin the evening but he also knew he would definitely have to ring them back. Everyone knew he wasn't on duty so no one would be calling him at this time of the night with good news about the station's chook raffle.

"Hi Ronnie, it's Clark, have you been trying to get me?"

"Yes Inspector, there's been an incident."

And the gig ended then and there.

It had only taken ten minutes for Clark to give Tom his apartment key and load the keyboard into the back of his twin cab. Then he was leaving the carpark, glad for once he hadn't even touched the free beer. Starting the car, Clark realised he hadn't even said goodnight to June, oh well, he'd catch up with her soon enough, the important thing for now was to refocus his brain away from the evening's music and onto his work.

Clark's route to the scene took him right through the centre of Wangaratta and out the other side but he drove quickly as there was hardly enough traffic on the road at that time of night to cause him any delay. He had not even been held up navigating the Waldara roadworks out of town and so, less than fifteen minutes later, he was already pulling off the road. He was not the first one there and parked up next to a solitary police car, its blue light flashing a lonely warning into the night. There were no streetlights this far out into the countryside, but he could vaguely see the outline of a bluestone farmhouse lit by a yellowish glow under the veranda. It was a big place, the sort you inherited from somebody who had come over from the old country years ago, and been pretty early off the boat. A federation property, build in the period, not the style.

On the gate, hard to read in the moonlight, a sign hung limply in the breezeless night air. Clark traced the thick gothic script with his finger; *Willow Cottage*. An inappropriate name, he thought to himself, given the house in no way fitted the description of a cottage, even if dawn could reveal the presence of a willow tree within the grounds.

Clark didn't recognise the young officer standing outside fiddling with his phone. He just shook his head, what are they teaching them at the Academy these days? Still, he thought, when he was at Glen Waverley a mobile phone was the size of a house brick and all it did was make phone calls, badly.

"Evening Constable, Inspector Clark Reynolds, what have we got here?"

"Uh, dead man sir. About fifty or sixty I guess, old anyway. A Donald McKay, the house owner. The wife has identified him, she's inside."

Clark's first impression of the young man was 'unimpressed.' He was a good detective if not perhaps a good policeman in the conventional sense, not quite text book enough for some tastes, but old fashioned enough to always present himself professionally. Clark was also a member of the rare breed of officers who had been promoted solely due to his ability, as evidenced by his enviable clearance rate, rather than his aptitude at police station politics. It also put him in the dubiously privileged position of knowing that, although he was barely forty himself, it was very unlikely he would ever be promoted again. Nonetheless, here he was with this young Constable Clot, or whatever his name was, new to the force, and no doubt hoping to be on his way up; first he'd have to have a few things explained to him. It was

Clark's duty. He would try not to raise his voice, try, but it may not work.

"Are you telling me she is inside, at a probable crime scene, unsupervised?"

"No," the constable defended himself, "the Sergeant's with her."

On reflection Clark realised he shouldn't have jumped to a negative conclusion about the young constable based solely on his possessing the same phone habit as the rest of his generation, and his inability to stand up straight. Was Clark just upset because his evening had been spoilt? On reflection maybe he should have had a beer after all.

"Okay. Well done. Is the doc on her way?"

"I don't think so sir. Couldn't reach her. She's not answering her phone. I've left a message on the surgery's voicemail, in case she checks it tonight."

"Constable, I happen to know she's not on call tonight, and I also happen to know how to reach her, only she's not going to thank me for it."

He stepped towards the front door.

The constable called after him. "I've called forensics, they aren't there but someone's coming down from Wodonga instead so it'll be a while before they get here," before defiantly adding inaudibly under his breath, "and I got that right too, didn't I."

He hoped his remark had not been heard when the inspector called back as if in reply, "Don't just stand there Constable, make yourself useful and go and have a look in the garage."

"What am I looking for in the garage?"

"Cars, how many cars are in the garage would be a good start."

The inside of the house matched its outside, stylish period features and big old dark brown furniture in the entrance hall. There were several unusual items as well, including an old brass umbrella stand shaped like an upturned partially opened umbrella and an art deco gilded mirror. The wallpaper was hand blocked, no doubt original. Everything had a pleasing patina from long age and use, the only concession to modernity being a sleek reverse cycle air-conditioner efficiently fighting the remains of the days heat, although even this had been carefully installed behind a lacework panel to partially conceal the jarringly incongruous modern plastic box. Everything was well cared for and clean except for a few footprints on the polished boards. To the right of the hallway was a formal dining room. The table was laid. The furniture looked as if it all came from a time when such items were the work of cabinetmakers, who like other craftsmen were members of guilds. The room was strangely populated by standard lamps of all sized and shapes. Some were beautiful cut glass oil lamps, Clark never doubted for a second that if called upon each would work perfectly. Directly in front of the entrance door stood a staircase wide enough to drive Clark's ute up, it could have probably supported the weight too. It was unusual to have a two-story farm house of that age in rural Victoria; the whole place said historic, perhaps even National Trust. Clark half expected there to be a little gift shop or at least a rack of postcards for sale by the front door.

He called out. "Sergeant?"

"In the kitchen, downstairs, back of the house."

Clark followed the voice, he recognised it belonged to Senior Sergeant Alice Dees and wondered if she sang, she would probably be a rich contralto if she did. He liked Alice, she was a good copper, knew what she's doing and already three quarters of the way to becoming an inspector herself.

A senior sergeant and barely thirty, almost unheard of. Everyone said Alice had been fast-tracked because she was indigenous of course but, well, what if it was true, would it really matter when she could do the job? It was probably better than the old system of having promotions based on what public school you went to anyway.

He entered the kitchen, traditionally decked out in polished timber and marble benchtops. The doorway looked directly at a proud display of vintage crockery, Spode china, all blue and white on an elegant Victorian dresser. There was even an old wood burning range above which hung an immaculate array of copper-bottomed pans. The room was large, well lit. Normally he would have labelled it as warm and functional, but today with the last of this Indian summer heat wave, stifling would have been a better description. There was nothing which would have looked out of place on one of those upmarket television cooking shows, the ones with a celebrity chef telling viewers how to cook authentic regional dishes, in a French accent as rich as the sauces, only this was the real thing, not a studio set.

There were two women seated at either side of the long bench table. Between them a pot of freshly brewed coffee steamed invitingly.

"Alice ?" Clark enquired.

The young police woman looked up. "Evening Sir, how was the gig?"

"You know, okay I guess, thanks. June was good, she always is. Anyway, Alice, what's the story here then?"

"This is Mrs Emma McKay. We're just having a coffee until her daughter gets here. I suggested she should stay with her tonight. The daughter's a local, she just lives in the middle of Wang, so she shouldn't be long. Mrs McKay found her husband upstairs at about seven. Nothing upstairs has been touched except I have confirmed he is deceased, not that I really had to under the circumstances as you'll see, he's lost a lot of blood. When I checked him, he was already cold, probably been dead for a while. The Doc may be able to say more but we can't get hold of her."

Clark looked at Mrs McKay. She had the obvious signs of shock but even with her smudged mascara was still a handsome woman. Dyed blond hair, neat and tidy in a bun. If her husband really was fifty or sixty she must have been much younger than him. His guess would be she was about his age, maybe a little older, a well-kept late forties. The couple must have been one of those May-September romances. She was well-dressed too, in a prim country-casual sort of way, a tailored checked shirt and RM Williams jeans.

Clark made his way over and poured himself a cup of coffee, uninvited. It was appropriately bitter.

"Mrs McKay, I'm very sorry for your loss. I will need to speak to you at some point but not necessarily now. Tomorrow perhaps."

Mrs McKay nodded to acknowledge him but said nothing.

Seeing there was no sugar on the table to take the edge off his coffee he placed the cup back down on the table and left the two women in the kitchen. Returning to the silence of the entrance hallway he made a phone call.

"Hello June, It's Clark here, Look I'm really sorry to ruin what's left of the evening but I'm in need of your professional help."

June's reply could just be heard above the noise of her car as it rumbled along an unsealed road. "I know, I've heard. See you in ten."

The upstairs of the house had a carpeted landing with rooms off in all directions. Only one door was ajar. Clark went in turning on the light carefully by flicking the switch with the end of his pen. It was a large bedroom, lots of chintz, all floral patterns and very feminine. The curtains were open. On the bed lay a shotgun; on the floor a man. Blood and mess were all over the headboard and the bed sheets. The man was in his underwear with his shirt and trousers tossed on to the floor next to the bed, his shoes and socks had been neatly placed under a bedside table. He could have been anything from late middle age to about seventy, overweight but not obese. If it wasn't for the bloody wound to his neck you could easily imagined he had just fallen out of bed.

Clark put on some latex gloves, and started opening drawers randomly, he wasn't sure why or what he was looking for. Apart from the shooting there was no sign the room had been ransacked, no indication that the murder had been part of a robbery, everything was too neat and tidy, undisturbed. He quickly found Mrs McKay's jewels inside an unlocked ornamental box within a drawer of one of the bedside tables; there were some rings, emeralds and diamonds maybe, lots of earrings. Clark found himself wondering why anyone needed so many earrings, after all she could only wear two at a time. There was also a double string of fresh-water pearls which looked like little pieces of puffed rice, only polished and shiny. He doubted it was her good stuff, all pretty enough, but nothing looked very valuable; not that Clark was a big buyer of women's jewellery. On the other bedside table sat Mr McKay's wallet. His credit cards were intact inside but there was no cash. Still, thought Clark, I don't seem to carry cash very often these days either, so its absence may not be significant. He also found a couple of Rolexes and what appeared to be some sort of old aviators watch marked Longines Weems. Like with the women's jewellery, Clark's areas of expertise didn't really extend into giving appraisals for men's watches, but he did know enough that they at least looked expensive. All told there were plenty of things about the bedroom you would not normally expect to find left behind at the scene of a burglary.

Clark removed his latex gloves and nipped into the en-suite to wash the powder off his hands. The damp towels left him trying to shake the water off into the handbasin, and rubbing them dry on his trousers. Clark was just thinking, 'why do the nicest houses always have the worst towels?' when he heard a noise behind him. He looked up into the mirror and saw the reflection of a girl in her early twenties standing behind him in the doorway. Clark ushered her back out of the room and onto the landing, shooing her with his arms as if herding a duckling. "I'm sorry but you can't be in here at the moment."

The girl was a younger version of her mother. She had the same bone structure, the same dyed blond bun.

"I just had to see for myself, I don't know why."

"Good evening, I am Inspector Reynolds and I'm… well I'm very sorry for your loss. Now I know this is a terrible time but while you are here do you mind answering a couple of preliminary questions. We can leave any formal statement for later, only there are a few things I'd like to know to get things started. Would it be alright, only I'd rather not bother your mother, not tonight."

She nodded.

"Firstly, you are Mr McKay's daughter?"

"Oh no." She paused. "Well sort of. I'm Sarah Roberts, and Donald is my stepfather. …He was my stepfather." She paused again but only momentarily whilst she took a few short breaths before continuing with her explanation. "Donald married my mother about five or six years ago. I was about 16 at the time, a bit late to start calling him Daddy."

"Nice man?"

"He's kind enough in his own way." She paused again before going on. "Good to Mother, and helped me out a bit here and there too, you know financially."

"A happy marriage then?"

"I think so, yes."

Clark noticed her voice had gone up a semi-tone, a subtle change but to his musician's ear one that was telling.

Clark stayed quiet, nodding to show he was still listening but giving her time to elaborate, an old trick, but one he found regularly worked, particularly when people were lying.

"Let me put it this way, my mother hasn't ever said anything to me and I think she would have, she normally lets everyone know when she's unhappy."

After another pause, she again broke the slightly awkward silence.

"Obviously, there have been a few arguments here and there, no marriage is perfect, is it, but nothing really bad that I know of."

Clark sensed it was time to change topic.

"And did your stepfather own a gun?"

"Yes, as far as I know. He used to anyway. At least two, a shotgun and a hunting rifle, maybe more. Donald did like to hurt things."

"But, not your mother?"

"No Inspector, not my mother"

Clark could hear it again, a slight change of pitch in her voice. What was it? The sound of tightly closing ranks perhaps. He recognised that particular melody having heard the song played once or twice before. Time to move on again, before she closed up completely. He made a quick mental note to ask around about the marriage later.

Clark stepped to one side so she could look into the room again.

"Is that his shotgun on the bed?"

Sarah peered in.

"It may be, I'm not very good with guns I'm afraid. My husband would know, they have gone shooting together a couple of times, but I've never really paid any notice. I don't really approve, not a farm girl you see."

"Would your mother know?"

"I wouldn't think so Inspector, if anything she's even worse than me with guns."

"So not a farm girl either then."

"Not before Donald. She always says everything smells of cow shit and eucalyptus, not her thing. It wasn't Donald's either really, he inherited this place from his Dad. He has always lived here. Mother and I used to joke about it and call it the Laird's Hoose."

"So, who owns the farm?"

"Well Donald owns it all, he owns it all for miles around, but unlike his father he has always had the farm managed. Pete King is the current manager; Donald hardly ever did anything himself here, he was always far too busy turning old money into lot's more money to do any actual farming. Property was Donald's thing. New housing developments called things like Lakeland Park Executive Estate. You probably know the sort of thing, endless split level brick veneer, mass housing for the soulless. I've always wondered how anyone could live in those houses without feeling they are a second rate set for the latest *Stepford Wives* remake. Still, he used to make good money though; there are just lots of bogans I guess, people who aspire to lifestyles instead of personalities."

Clark heard her rather condescending speech, noted the judgemental manner. His instinct was to defend those she had dismissed by saying something about it being the best they could afford, instead his training kicked in and he picked up on one particular phrase.

"You said, *'used to'* make money."

"Did I? I only meant he won't be making any more money now, will he?"

Clark listened carefully, picking up the melodies in her speech, the subtle variations of tone. He hadn't heard enough to be certain, and yet, he had the sense it was not what she really meant at all. He would have to check out the business' finances in the morning; see if Donald was still making money.

"And finally, for now, can you think of any reason your stepfather would have to harm himself, or of anyone who may have wanted to harm him?"

"Well, he wasn't shall we say a well-liked man. He cheated a few too many people over the years, but no one particular springs to mind. No one who would actually do that to him anyway."

"Have there ever been any death threats?"

"I really wouldn't know Inspector."

"And suicide?"

"Well, I suppose you can never be 100% certain, can you? But no, he wasn't really the type; liked himself too much."

"Thank you, shall we go and see if your mother is alright?"

They descended the staircase together, Clark pausing momentarily as he noticed two empty picture hooks on the wall.

"What normally hangs here?"

"There are a couple of old pictures, landscapes. One is of the house actually. There are a few other pictures around if you are interested." She stopped in mid-sentence. "Do you think that's why he was murdered, for the pictures?"

Clark gave her a, "it's something we will look into," by way of an uncommitted reply, before adding he'd never heard of an art theft being accompanied by the brutal shooting of a near naked man. "So," he concluded, "I very much doubt it."

Sarah nodded before changing topic and starting again. "Inspector, there is always the Richardson girl, do you know about her?" She made it seem as if she was almost embarrassed to bring it up, as if it was all somehow too distasteful to mention. Clark wasn't fooled, he was starting to get a good read on her. He did however have some vague recollection, Richardson, a name he knew from somewhere; maybe a file he had once seen or read, an old case, not his, from a couple of years ago.

"I think I know the name, but please remind me."

"The Richardsons," she started, "have worked on the farm for, well, I don't know, let's say a long time. Since before my mother married Donald certainly. Their daughter May Richardson is about my age, common girl but sometimes we did a bit of riding together. Riding is about the only thing I miss about living here really. I still have a horse. Anyway, May did some cleaning work here a couple of years ago. We, the family, all think she stole one of my stepfather's things, a little porcelain figurine of a boy with a sheep. A horrid kitsch little thing actually, not even worth ten bucks. Well, of course, she claimed she hadn't stolen it and pretended we had just lost it, or something. We told the police but they couldn't prove anything so she just left. It all got very ugly for a while, threats of all sorts. They aren't in our social circle you understand, but there is still bad blood if we bump into them, and you know rural families, it's a small community and you always see people, even those you'd rather not. I don't think they even work on the farm these days, I think her dad works at one of the supermarkets in town, but I think they still rent the same cottage."

June arrived shortly; she hadn't had time to change out of her stage outfit. Unselfconsciously she rolled up her skirt and slipped into a disposable coverall at the side of the road. Clark led her inside so she could begin her examination of the body.

"There he is, our murder victim."

"Aren't I the one who say's if it is a murder or not."

"Not in this case," Clark informer her.

"Go on, I know you're dying to show off."

"It's simple," explained Clark, "the shotgun hasn't got any empty cartridges in it, someone's taken them out already, and I suggest, that unidentified someone was alive at the time and therefore not the victim. I've heard of people trying to make a murder look like a suicide but not the other way round."

"Unless," suggested June, "it's a life insurance thing."

"All I'm saying is," said Clark trying hard not to sound as if he was indeed showing off, "you do your examination but you'll only prove I'm right."

It was another hour and a half before the forensic unit arrived. By the time Clark had spoken to them it was well past two and he was fading fast. On his way out he stopped for a last look in the hall. Something was bothering him about the house but he couldn't quite put his finger on it. He reminded forensics to take plenty of pictures, hopefully it would come to him when he looked at them tomorrow, after he had a good night's sleep.

Chapter 2 - Wednesday Morning

Oh, please have some pity
I'm all alone in this big city
I tell you I'm just a lonesome babe in the wood
So lady, be good to me

George and Ira Gershwin

Denning Mathews drove a large four-wheel-drive Mercedes; it had never been off road, well not unless you counted his annual weekend to the snow. His suit was a bespoke double-breasted pinstripe, a little flashy for most professions but in Denning Mathew's world it was just right. Denning was an art advisor. It was his job to find rich people with more money than taste. His ideal client being somebody who already owned several desirable and collectible works of art who he could convince it was in their own best interest to sell one or two and then buy some other desirable and collectible works instead, all the while taking a healthy percent cut. He largely worked on PT Barnum's business principle of sixty fools being born hourly, much like almost everyone else in the art world, and having the great Mr Barnham's business ethics, as a completely unprincipled scoundrel, it was perhaps unsurprising how successful he was in his chosen field. Money loved art it seemed, even during the Covid pandemic he had manage to make a bit of coin here and there, and who was he to turn away his share at the best of times. Notably he had recently started working with an heiress from a well-known hotel owning family who had just discovered the Australian Impressionists, only one hundred years or so too late. If he could find anything from the Heidelberg School then Denning Mathews would be able to trade-up his girlfriend, if not his Mercedes.

Today he was alone in his pretentiously exclusive gallery. The leather chairs remained empty, there were no appointments in his diary. His research assistant, Dr Zara Winman PhD, Fellow of the Art Association of Australia and New Zealand, was working from home. She often did these days, chasing down the missing links in a picture's provenance. A full provenance, one which can remove any doubt about a picture's authenticity, can greatly increase its auction price. It was largely in this way Dr Zara earned back her considerable salary several times over each year, as well as adding a touch of academic expert respectability to the place. On normal days there was also the obligatory snooty young receptionist seated at a desk near the front door but as there were no viewings scheduled, Denning had given her the day off, insisted actually. He wasn't going to pay her to just sit there and update her Facebook page on his time. This morning, he was not in a particularly good mood, the café across the road's latte tasted like a cappuccino and to add insult to that most grievous injury they had also run out of doughnuts. He really didn't know why he went there, if he didn't fancy the barista a little bit, with her broad smile and extra-long legs, well, then he would have definitely gone elsewhere.

So, Denning found himself alone in his gallery wondering what the morning would bring and day dreaming about the barista who was much tastier than her coffee. He had not been alone for long though before a young woman knocked on the door holding a small brown paper parcel under her arm.

He walked over to the door, just slowly enough to get a good look. She was an attractive young blond, smartly dressed in a casual going to a Sunday afternoon Toorak house party sort of way, just Denning's type. His day was looking up already. He decided to open the door.

"Good morning, can I help you?" He greeted her with fake charm oozing precipitously. There was the slightest affectation of an exotic eastern European accent, Hungarian, maybe Slavic.

"Possibly, I'm looking to sell a couple of pictures."

Denning would have much preferred her to have said "buy a couple of pictures," he had more than enough in stock at the moment as it was. In Denning's line of work, it wasn't as if he could have a quick 10% off sale to reduce his excess inventory, art couldn't ever be discounted like last season's fashion, that would shatter its hard-earned illusion of value. Still, he supposed, a casual walk-in buyer, at this hour of the morning, was a bit too much to hope for.

There was a slight chink in the charm offensive as he explained to the girl, "I don't really buy from artists I'm afraid. I can give you some names if you like, but it's not really my thing, new art, I mean."

The girl laughed. If Denning had been as good with people as he thought he was, then he may have spotted he was himself now being played. "I don't mean I painted them," she said, almost adding a, "silly," on the end but stopped herself in time with the realisation doing so would have been one step too far. Instead, she simply continued, "I think you'll want to see these. I'm told they are rather good."

Over the years Denning Mathews had lost count of the number of times he had been offered pictures painted by some unknown's grandfather; paintings which, just because they had spent a few years in an attic, were supposed to have magically acquired an increased desirability. Art just didn't work like that, age didn't equate to value, or technical quality to worth for that matter. Still, she was rather attractive, and it wasn't as if he was busy. He decided he may as well humour her a bit longer. Long enough to get her phone number at least.

"Well, why don't we have a little gander darling."

He led her inside, locking the security door tightly behind them. In the back room was a narrow table, probably 18th century French, definitely walnut. A nice piece, good enough to seem impressive in the gallery space but without being too expensive to use for daily work. She placed her parcel on the table and Denning made a joke about his love of brown paper packages tied up with string. The remark showed his age and the girl clearly didn't catch the reference.

Denning hesitated, as if making a silent wish, before opening the parcel. Inside, cushioned only by being wrapped loosely in an old tea towel, were two small pictures. Both oils, and both appeared at a quick glance to be of excellent quality. The first was around 9 inches by 5 inches painted on a wooden panel which Denning presumed to be the lid of old cigar box, the import stamp on its back being in Spanish and including the word, *Havana*. The painting itself, a landscape, purported to be by Charles Condor, certainly it was signed and dated, CC '89. On the frame a brass plaque named the picture as *Dandenong Summer Day* but gave no additional attribution as to the artist. It was well executed with subtle, almost pastel, tones. Yes, thought Denning, the style was right and there was no obvious reason to doubt it. As always, he found himself thinking not about the quality of the picture but about its market value. If it was listed under Charles Condor in a catalogue, particularly the 1889 9x5 Melbourne Exhibition Catalogue, it was worth a mint, if not, early Condor's, those before his later European adventures, seldom came to the market, making it still an extremely good find. Maybe, coming to think of it, a bit too good a find. Genuine Condor's don't just knock on your door at ten past nine on a Wednesday morning, not in Denning's experience anyway. Oh well, whether it was genuine or not, and he couldn't be 100% sure either way, it was definitely good enough to pass any amateur's inspection and in his line that was all that really mattered. He wasn't aware of other paintings Charles Condor had initialled CC rather than signing but that detail was something the authenticating expert could discuss later. Perhaps it was the sign of a good forgery, some little quirk to give the experts something to debate, something to prove by its exception, the picture was genuine. On second thoughts he would avoid showing the picture to any museums and stick to the private investors market, that way he should be fine. The initials CC could stand for Charles Condor or Charlie Chaplin for all he cared, the only important thing was if it could get him a decent percentage.

The second picture was a little trickier. Again, a small oil painting but this time completely unsigned although the frame had a placard stating *The Willows – F. McCubbin*, and it was true at first glance there was indeed something about the style which hinted at Frederick McCubbin. A very promising picture of a two-story bluestone farmhouse viewed from a low angle, a point of view rather reminiscent of McCubbin's painting *The Mountain Cottage* of 1915. Possibly, truth be told, too reminiscent, even down to having some scattered poultry in the foreground. Denning had seen several pictures by McCubbin at auction over the last few years and been considerably outbid every time, was this picture going to make up for those previous disappointments? Only, there was something, somehow not quite right about the clouds. Now, if he could prove McCubbin had ever been in the same room as this picture he'd be laughing, only there were those gloomy somewhat blocky clouds. Apart from the sky, which after all he could always say had been unsympathetically restored, the overall technique was not quite romantic enough for a McCubbin. The trees and building were good technically, maybe even good enough, but it wasn't quite right when you looked above the horizon, which compositionally was in an unusual place anyway. To Denning's eye, there was just nothing spontaneous in the brushwork, the strokes were all too short and a little too carefully measured. It reminded him of those old paint-by-numbers kits and if there was one thing you could never accuse Frederick McCubbin of it was being a bit of a paint-by-numbers artist; overly sentimental perhaps, but never formulaic. A copy of a McCubbin maybe, but the real thing, extremely unlikely even to his eye. A pity really. He decided he'd better stop looking so hard, just in case he could prove without a doubt it definitely was a fake. Sometimes in his line of work it was better not to know. Maybe if he just hinted strongly, he had a Condor and a "probable" McCubbin to a couple of his more stupid clients, not giving any guarantees you understand, one of them would bite; he would sell them as a pair, the Condor lending its weight to the authenticity of the other. Yes, that sounded like a plan, keep them together and he'd do well out of this little duo.

All up, not a bad morning's work, and it wasn't even ten o'clock yet. He'd better not let Zara see them, after all there was no need to check the provenance on these, and the last thing he needed was her to tear their limited credibility to bits on the spot. Still, he could smell there was money to be made here. It was just a minor shame at least one, if not both of them, was a fake.

June White MD, part time jazz singer and full time Fellow of the Royal College of Pathologists had a busy day ahead of her. It had been well after two in the morning when she had climbed into her bed and despite her best hopes the night before she had once again found herself tucked up alone. Where the hell was Clark anyway? She really had to sort that man out at some point. Currently she had half a wardrobe at his apartment, and he had a spare sock drawer and a tooth brush at her house. His only concession to a real commitment was to have left his baby-grand in her living room because his own flat was too small. It was an arrangement which was all getting a little old, and she wasn't getting any younger, as her mother kept reminding her.

Maybe she'd bring it up again today, she would be seeing him later in the morning after the post-mortem. Then again, perhaps, her mortuary wouldn't make for the best setting. First, she would finish the PM, take her report round and invite him over for tea. She could bring up their relationship then, if he was in the right mood. Yes, she thought, I'll do something simple like mushroom pasta, something homely that said it doesn't have to be a special occasion we can just be comfortable like any other couple and have a nice evening together. A glass of Tempranillo maybe, the one she and Clark had bought on their weekend trip in the King Valley, that always got him in a good mood. Then she would be able to slip living arrangements into the conversation. Thinking about it, wasn't the lease on his flat coming up soon anyway? It was beginning to sound like a plan.

First though she had to sort out Mr McKay's murder. She was already sure it was murder from her initial examination last night. Apart from anything else it was almost impossibly difficult to discharge both barrels of a full-length double-barrelled shotgun into yourself. Add to that the fact suicides rarely shot themselves in the throat; coming to think of it, it was amazing his head was still attached to the rest of his body after having been shot at such close range. Death would have been instantaneous so the fact was if he had somehow done it to himself, there on his own bed, and somehow dropped the gun as he fell, them wouldn't the gun have fallen closer to the body and not been thrown clear? It was true she would have expected there to have been more blood but it was definitely a murder, as she had told Clark within seconds of first seeing the body. She was as sure of that as, well, she was sure of Clark. She still had to do all the rest of the post mortem procedure and finish the job of course, she would try and keep an open mind, that was good science. It sometimes bothered her on the days when as a pathologist, she was discovering how people died, she earned more money than when she worked as a doctor, trying to keep them alive in the first place. Something didn't feel right about that, but she was professional enough to always do both jobs, and do both to her best; today she would earn her fee.

The car trip into the office only took eleven minutes, she would remind Clark her house was in a better location than his flat later, and she had a garden too, much better for kids. On second thoughts, maybe she shouldn't be talking about kids at this stage, no need to be channelling her mother, better to save that chat for another day.

Passing the hospital's drive-through Covid testing marquee June couldn't help herself channelling her mother again by wondering if after the pandemic they would hire it out as a wedding pavilion. She really would have to speak to Clark soon, this persistent train of thought was starting to get ridiculous.

All the carparking near the hospital had already been taken, it always was early in the morning with relatives visiting their loved ones on their way to work. She however, as a senior member of staff, had a reserved spot alongside the other doctors and surgeon's cars. Her convertible Audi slotting in among the rest; a neat row of gleaming luxury.

The Pathology Department, June's location for the morning, was located appropriately in a dead-end corner of the building. During June's tenure it had moved several times as the hospital had undergone repeated redevelopments, always, or so it appeared to June, within earshot of a workman's jackhammer. She would have been the first to admit she didn't really need to be located anywhere better. There was certainly no requirement to provide any peace and quiet for the department's unfortunate customers to enjoy during their recovery. Still, it did annoy her the morgue was tucked in a corner where the smell lingered due to the sub-standard ventilation in that part of the building. There were certainly days when she would have liked to have been able to open a window. She was sure if the hospital administrator's office was next to hers the poor ventilation would be fixed within the week. More than once she had wondered whether other people could smell death on her, just like the fishmonger who always smelt of his produce. She made a mental note to wash her hair before Clark came round tonight; maybe she'd wash it twice.

Her technician, the wonderfully organised and helpful Mrs Pratibha Patil, had already made sure Mr McKay was correctly positioned on the table and was, even as June arrived, taking swabs of some white residue from under the fingernails of his left hand. The camera next to the pathology table suggested she had already done all the preliminary photographs as well. There was a dish of sterile instruments and a roll of green towelling in place on a stainless-steel trolley. Everything was ready for her to start. All she needed was to scrub and put on her gown, hat, gloves and of course yet another surgical mask. Like the entire population of the State she had worn more than enough of those over the past few months.

As she prepared herself, she chatted casually with Pratibha.

"The thing is," said Pratibha "Bejay is looking for a place to do his year 10 school work experience. It's only a week and I sort of told him I'd fix it for him here at the hospital."

June wasn't sure what the official policy on such things was, but Pratibha was the best assistant she had worked with, so she didn't want to say no. June therefore heard herself say, "I'll have a word with admin; as long as he doesn't expect to be assisting me in a post-mortem or administering drugs to patients, I'm sure we'll be able to sort something out." June wasn't the sort of person to keep score when helping people normally but as her mother said, "after all darling, what is the point of having people owe you a favour if you're not going to occasionally call one in."

Pratibha thanked her adding, "that would be great of you."

"No problem. Okay, let's get on with it, any impressions before I start? Any bruising come up overnight?"

"Nothing inconsistent with falling over, it doesn't look like he was assaulted or in a fight."

"Did anyone tell you he was found on a mattress?"

"If that's the case, he didn't fall on it, there are some bruises."

"You've taken photos?" It wasn't really a question; June knew from past experience she would have.

"And swabs. I've even found a few fibres in his hair you should take a look at."

"Good, I suppose it's time to get started."

The post-mortem examination wasn't actually scheduled to start until ten o'clock, that was the official timing anyway. The Department always scheduled things to allow the police to attend if they wanted to. June knew Clark wouldn't so she could make an early start, give herself plenty of time.

Clark was feeling a little guilty at having broken his promise to cook Tom's breakfast by shooting out the door almost as soon as the alarm clock stopped, but as Tom had decided to stay for a few more days during the school holidays, he would make it up to him once he was on top of this wretched murder case.

The early start meant that Clark arrived at the police station well before the morning shift began, he liked to get into the office early sometimes, show he still could if it was necessary. One day, he decided, he should even try to get to the station before Sergeant Alice Dees did. Somehow, he suspected, that try as he may he would be unlikely to succeed. She was still young enough and keen enough to be trying to prove her worth to those higher up the food chain than him. Clark had already made his assessment of her abilities: positive on all counts, he had even put her name forward for a commendation earlier in the year.

He was greeted in the carpark by the usual selection of press representatives, shouting out their normal array of questions.

"Inspector, what can you tell us about the shooting?"

"Are you treating it as murder?"

"Can you confirm it was Donald McKay?"

"Inspector, do you have any suspects at this stage?"

It was a small press corps and Clark recognised most of them; Anna from the ABC Regional News, his old mate Tony from the local paper, and that annoying girl with fake eyelashes from commercial TV whose name he could never remember, Catherine, Caitlyn, Karen maybe, something like that anyway, perhaps. He would have to say something.

"All I can say at this point is that we are treating it as a suspicious death."

The reporters began calling out again.

"I'm sorry. We are already pursuing various lines of enquiry and there will be a press conference later, until then I'm afraid I can't answer any questions. Thank you."

He walked past in a strange dance acknowledging Tony with a half nod while at the same time endeavouring to ignore the few final questions.

At the reception desk was Sergeant Ronald Tutt, not so much old school as pre-school, a veteran closing in fast on his well-earned retirement; no-nonsense, incorruptible.

"Morning Ronnie, is she in yet?"

She was, Alice Dees was busy arranging desks and setting up an incident room for the daily morning briefing. So, he thought to himself, Alice does have a flaw. He didn't know if it was alright to allow himself a brief moment of smugness at having found it; she doesn't delegate enough, a sergeant shouldn't be shifting all the desks by herself. If he had time, he'd have a word with her about it, and with that thought of delegation, Inspector Clark Reynolds started a mental process of allocating the day's jobs.

Firstly; there were the key individual statements, Mrs McKay, her daughter (he'd forgotten the name but it would come back to him, Sarah something), and hadn't she said something about the family having a cleaner. Well, they were all women so he'd get Alice to speak to them, she'd probably get them to say more. No, on second thought he'd speak to the mother first while Alice could see the daughter. They were probably both at the daughter's house this morning anyway. That way they could interview them both at the same time, and importantly, separate them.

Then there was the happy marriage angle. That sounded like a good gossipy sort of investigation. Hear-say was not something admissible in a court of course, but at this early stage of an investigation rumours could be very useful. Alice could do those enquiries after they had seen the family. She could go around the neighbours, get the low down. The daughter was married so there was at least a husband. He'd speak to him at some point but it probably wasn't a priority. No doubt there were other family members living nearby, sisters, aunts, brothers and so on. He'd add Mr Sarah, whatever his name was, onto that list and allocate those interviews later.

So, thought Clark, all that's left Mr McKay's business dealings and the legal bits around the will. Who stands to gain what is always good to know; and there was still something odd about the house at the back of his mind. Maybe he'd do the legal bits and get Alice to have a good look round the house while she was out there talking to the neighbours. The more he thought about it the surer he was there was something he had missed at the house and hopefully Alice, with her fresh pair of eyes, would spot it for him. If not then he could always go back at some point himself.

He should also speak to June about the post mortem. She should be finished sometime around lunchtime. It was fairly doubtful there was anything interesting; even he could see the guy had been shot, but if there was something else as well, it could be important to know.

Oh, he had almost forgot, the Richardson girl. He should read the case file, and maybe go and interview her or her family.

So, thinking it through slowly, he and Alice should be able to get a handle on this one and there was no need to involve anyone else at this stage. After the two of them had made all those initial inquiries, they could take things from there. Obviously, if something unexpected cropped up then they would need someone else, like one of the fraud boys to look over the books, but for now he'd leave it on hold, as at this preliminary stage in the case there were plenty of other things to get on with first.

He decided he had better have a quick word with the Super before saying his bit at the briefing. Then he and Alice could get on with the investigation.

Superintendent Edward Edwards, 'Teddy' to his old friends and fellow members of the bowls club, was a good boss and rarely interfered with any ongoing investigations. It helped that Teddy and Clark had known each other for a long time; back when Clark had first transferred to the North Eastern Region from Melbourne as a young constable the then equally younger Sergeant Edwards had been something of a mentor to him. Nowadays, as long as Clark kept him in the loop Teddy looked after Clark and his team by letting Clark handle the day to day running of cases in his own way. It was a simple arrangement, but one which suited them both.

The superintendent was seated at his desk. He was slightly balding and a little overweight, the type to play Father Christmas at the local fete if it wasn't for his eyes; his eyes displayed a predator's sharpness. For all his superficial jocularity few who were caught by the Teddy's gaze failed to take him seriously, and those who did never did so a second time. He was currently studying a computer spreadsheet and jotting down figures onto a yellow sticky note. His office door was open, as it normally was. Clark tapped and entered.

He looked up, acknowledging his inspector with a simple, "Clark."

"Morning Sir, I've come to fill you in about this McKay murder last night."

"Tell me what you need."

Clark smiled. It was typical Teddy, never a "what are you doing?" always a "what do you need?" with the positive and supportive assumption Clark was always doing the right thing and he, as Clark's boss, would therefore just try to find a way to help him do it easier.

"I'd like Alice for the day to start with and we'll come up with a plan after doing all the basic interviews; relatives, friends, neighbours, you know the sort of thing."

"I want you to use young Luca Bastoni on this one."

'Now,' thought Clark, 'this is new, Teddy always allows me to pick my own team.' But instead of saying so, or pointing out Alice Dees was an experienced detective whereas Luca Bastoni was a very inexperienced uniform officer, he found himself instead saying, "I'd rather have Alice, a lot of the key characters are women and, you know, the feminine touch."

"Alright, but take Luca around with you too, I think he'll be useful on this one."

Luca Bastoni was an unusual addition to the police force. Recruited straight from university, unlike most officers these days who don't join until they have gained at least some life experience, he had a double degree in pure and applied mathematics. For some such an unusual qualification for a policeman would have been remarkable enough in itself, but what really set the senior ranks talking about the young constable, still only six months in from his initial training, was his father, a leading power broker in the Victorian

Government, the Honourable Joe Bastoni, MP for Snowy River.

Clark hadn't been introduced to the stations latest young officer yet and found himself hoping it was not the phone fiddling new constable from the previous night. But more worrying than that, as he was already well aware of who Luca's father was, was the quiet alarm bell just starting to sound in his head. "Teddy, is there anything I should know?"

"No, no, no, just take him along and let's see if he's useful, when we're dealing with a family like the McKay's a few family connections can prove to be worth their weight in gold."

"One thing, I just told the media people there would be a press conference later this morning."

"I've already sorted one out, you'll have to be there of course. We'll do it at half eleven so be back here to see me before then."

The back seat of the twin-cab ute gave Luca Bastoni little in the way of leg room. His suggestion Clark put the keyboard on the pick-up's tray had been met without either comment or action, and so Luca squashed himself in and hoped the trip wasn't going to take too long. It didn't.

Cramped in the back as he was Luca was glad to be on the case, excited even. It was his first murder and a successful conclusion would without doubt be a feather in his cap. Up to this point his most impressive collar had been a car thief who stole late 20th century models because as he had explained when Luca arrested him, "they're easier to repair." He had said this in such a way Luca was left wondering why he would be stealing broken cars in the first place. Surely, he had thought to himself, you didn't need to be a criminal mastermind to realise cars which did not need repairing would be easier for the get-away. Now he had a shot at working a murder case and outwitting a real criminal, just like they did on N.C.I.S. Major cases were what got you noticed, he told himself, they help your career. It also gave him the opportunity to work with Inspector Reynolds, the senior detective had a formidable reputation and their brief meeting outside Willow Cottage the night before had not gone well. Now he had another chance and was determined to make the most of it, a positive word from an officer of Inspector Reynold's standing and he could probably get out of uniform permanently, it would at least get him a place on the next detective training course. His first placement after graduating last year had been to spend time at a Covid checkpoint up on the New South Wales border. Luca had no intention of spending his entire career doing those sorts of mundane jobs, the occasional shift of crowd control outside the MCG had been bad enough, not to mention the ugly scenes ungluing an environmental activist from the Southgate bridge. No, Luca wasn't the type to be happy in a traffic patrol car driving up and down the Hume highway handing out speeding fines. Work for your run of the mill sort of copper but not, he thought to himself, suitable for him. Luca was going places and if his dad had to pull a few strings to open some doors, well wasn't that the way of the world?

There was one minor drawback with this current assignment, it meant working with Sergeant Alice Dees. Luca didn't like her. He didn't really know why, but he didn't. He hoped it wasn't because she was aboriginal. He'd hate to be considered a racist, he certainly didn't think of himself that way. It was true a few of his friends made the odd colourful joke, it was just their way, but he never did. He even pulled them up on it occasionally when he felt their banter had crossed the line. Equally he hoped it wasn't because she was a woman. His best friend Toni was a girl after all, and that must prove something. And the more he thought about it, the more he convinced himself it wasn't his fault, there was no way he was biased or bigoted, the problem was with Alice herself, she was too, well, the only word he could think of was, intense. Just one of those things, he told himself, you can't get on with everyone, and it takes all sorts, that's just how things are.

Inspector Reynolds and Alice were sitting in the front of the ute, chatting earnestly about something to do with music. It was obvious they got on well enough. Luca decided if he had to impress the inspector he would just pretend for a few days. I'll call it *pretending for promotion*, he said to himself, there's nothing wrong in it, all part of the game, and who knows, as she gets to know me, she might even lighten up a bit.

Sarah Roberts' house in Wangaratta was one of those gorgeous 1920's brick properties backing onto the park near the centre of town. Clark quickly noted the bull nosed veranda, period stained-glass entrance and attractive wrought ironwork. It was a corner block with a small but well-established low maintenance garden and no doubt plenty of other desirable features. Clark realised he had been spending too much time at real estate offices; what should he do about his lease? Maybe he'd speak to June about it later, move in with her; get a dog. He'd always wanted a dog. It was something to think about anyway.

He knocked on the door. Emma McKay answered. She was still in her dressing gown, maybe unable to get up and face the world, maybe all an act. A heightened sense of suspicion can be both a detective's best asset and also their curse.

"Good morning Mrs McKay, I don't know if you remember me from last night."

"Of course I do Inspector, how are you?"

"I was just coming to ask you the same thing. This is Constable Bastoni and you already know Sergeant Dees. Would it be alright if I had a word with you while the Sergeant speaks to your daughter?"

"I'm sorry Inspector, my daughter has had to go out, she won't be back until this evening."

"In that case, if everything is alright, perhaps you and I could have a word while the Constable and my Sergeant go and have a look around at your house?"

Mrs McKay spent a moment before replying. When she did it was not to Clark.

"Constable, are you Joe's boy?"

Luca had expected to have to take a back seat, just observing the discussion, but now, given the chance to be involved, he stepped forward saying, "you know my father?"

"Oh yes, rather well. I know you too, only I haven't seen you since, well you must have been a teenager. My first husband and I used to come around regularly to stay with your parents."

Luca thought momentarily, frowned and then smiled. A penny had dropped and he had made the connection.

"Oh, you're Sarah's mum, and I remember Sam too of course, used to go fishing with dad, terrible moustache. I still keep in touch with Sarah you know, well I see her on her Facebook. All her paintings and photos of her dog, and her stupid three-legged cat, wait a minute…er…Mr…Mr. Sniggle? Where is Sarah?”

“Mr Sniffle, and I was just explaining to the Inspector, Sarah’s out I’m afraid.”

“Sarah Waters; small world.”

“You know she’s Sarah Roberts these days, married Colin Roberts.”

“Oh yes, wish I’d been able to get to the wedding, Bali I believe. I’ve seen the photos, looked amazing. I’ve saw them about out walking their dog. I almost stopped to say hello but didn’t want to be late for my shift, it’s a new posting. I was sort of surprised in a way because, I thought, well I don’t know if I should say this really, but I always had a feeling, after she went off to do her art thing at university, none of us would ever see her again. I always pictured her in some artists slum in Paris.”

“They’ve been living here 12 months now, moved in during the start of the lock-down. Now that was an adventure I must say, couldn’t get a removalist for love nor money.”

“I see Colin regularly of course. Only last week he was, at some party funder of my Dad’s, and he was talking about going to the MSO with Sarah at the weekend. He invited me to a party next week actually.”

“The party was supposed to be their sort of house warming anniversary barbeque do, a get-together to make up for not having a proper party last year when they moved in.”

“That’s just like Queen Sarah, a real house warming and an official one later,” joked Luca. “So, I suppose the party is going to be here.”

“They were having it in the garden, it’s cancelled now of course.” She sounded regretful, almost as if she didn’t understand why they had cancelled the party just because of her husband’s death, after all it would have been a good day.

"Well," said Luca "I'm sure I'll catch-up with Sarah soon, I'm just down the road myself these days. Like I said, small world."

"Small town anyway."

Luca had always been in a privileged position from being raised as part of a select network of influential people. He decided to see if he could use that here to his advantage and keep the conversation going with him at the forefront, but before he could Mrs McKay turned to Clark explaining, "Sam, your Constable's father's friend was my first husband Inspector. He died in a car accident about seven years ago. First Sam, now Donnie…" Then turning back, she continued, "how is your mother anyway, I haven't seen her for ages, I should give her a call."

"Oh, you know, as embarrassingly wacky as ever. Still doing her charity stuff and causing a bit of a stir."

Clark who had been carefully observing the conversation took the opportunity to interrupt with, "Maybe if I can come in and talk while the Sergeant and Luca go to your house for another look around."

"Alice," he said passing her some keys, "you take my car and I'll phone the station for a lift."

"It's ok sir," interrupted Luca, "I really am literally round the corner."

"Really?" observed Mrs McKay. "Policemen must be paid far too much if you can afford to live round here."

Mrs McKay led Inspector Reynolds inside and into a large open plan living area. The contrast between her own and her daughter's house was marked, everything here was new and aseptic apart from a small number of antiques displayed not as actual items of household furniture but more like statues in an art gallery, arranged for their aesthetic effect. There was also a curious mirrored sculpture. The pictures on the walls were modern pop-art prints and aggressive angular abstractions. The room was dominated by an enormous television set and two uncomfortable looking Bauhaus style leather and chrome couches carefully positioned to give the best views of the screen. One wall of the room was lined with books, mostly cheap paperbacks, the books arranged with colour coordinated spines to be admired, not read. The back of the room opened onto an outside living space through French windows. Much of the backyard was a building site in the process of being renovated by the addition of an entertaining area, comprised of a paved terrace, a fashionable fire pit and an unnecessarily large barbeque, all shaded by the only mature tree in the whole garden. At the bottom of the block sat a sort of granny-flat building acting as Sarah's painting studio. It had obviously been carefully positioned to completely prevent any views into next door's backyard and by doing so it turned the garden into a little private oasis in the centre of town.

The interview itself only lasted about twenty minutes, during which time Clark learnt only one thing which could prove useful; she had spent the day alone shopping but did see her husband for lunch in the arts centre cafe. Other than that, she revealed nothing, leaving Clark with the impression there was something important he was not being told. Maybe, he thought, he should have asked her to come to the station after all for a formal interview, but in Clark's experience there was usually an inverse correlation between how formal the interview was and the amount actually said. He asked her a range of other typical questions of course, but, because she was both the grieving widow and a murder suspect, Clark didn't push her too hard. He may have to later, if he got something worth pushing with, but not at this stage. At this point he would just have to accept her half-truths and look elsewhere for something more concrete.

In the car on the way back to the office he was annoyed with himself. He knew Alice would have got more out of Mrs McKay and regretted he had insisted on doing this one himself. If only he had trusted his original instinct and let Alice interview the women the investigation may have taken a bigger step forward. It couldn't be helped now.

Clark put on some music, Charlie Parker, *Mohawk*. The ideas in his head were coming fast and furiously. There was little shape linking them to any underlying stories but he had enough glances of a melody flitting in and out of view at the corner of his eye to let him know there was more going on than there seemed to be. It was often like that early in a case; bebop policework.

He phoned the station and was answered by the desk officer.

"Ronnie, it's Clark. A couple of things. Can you look up the May Richardson case file and put a print-out of it on my desk, along with her parent's current contact details. And can you get someone to find out the details of Mr McKay's property business and give it to Alice when she gets in, she'll know what to do with it. Thanks. Oh, and phone me when the forensics report or PM comes in, I asked them to CC me on my email but they never do. And one more thing Ronnie, can you remind Alice to run the serial number on the shotgun through the system. Knowing her she's probably done it already of course, but we do need to confirm what comes up, just in case it wasn't his gun."

The Wangaratta to Yarrawonga Road ran almost due north past an ever-increasing number of hobby-farm subdivisions and out into the rural area around Peechelba. It was a good road, straight enough to be easy to lose track of your speed on. Before arriving at Peechelba, a junction turned off to the left and out towards the tranquil Killawarra Forest and Warby Ranges. It was a good spot for a picnic, or if you had time, to pitch a tent. Many people did, although this summer, because of the Covid-19 restrictions, there had been considerably fewer than in other years. Of those visitors who did stop to enjoy the tranquillity, few would have known much about the area's darker history. In 1865 Peechelba had seen the final showdown between the authorities and the infamous bushranger Dan 'Mad Dog' Morgan, a home invasion incident which had also featured a baby, Christina MacPherson, the same Christina MacPherson who years later when she had grown up inspired Banjo Paterson to write Waltzing Matilda. The Killawarra Forest picnic ground itself had not always been an idyllic retreat, during the second World War, it had been used as an internment camp for Italian migrants, although of course in its defence there are plenty of less scenic places to spend a war. Accounts from the period suggest that the internees had a comparatively easy time of it from the sympathetic part timers assigned to guard them.

Additionally, and more recently occurring than either of those historical incidents, at one of its most prominent addresses, Willow Cottage, there had been the discovery of a dead body.

Willow Cottage looked even better in sunlight; Alice was able to admire the roses in the garden that the night before she had only been able to smell. The front door was locked with an official crime scene notice attached asking people not to enter. She unlocked it and went inside. Alice shuddered, was it the air-conditioner which had been left running overnight or the sense something terrible had happened there. Perhaps, she had to consider, she wouldn't have felt so uncomfortable if the murder had taken place in town, in the social housing near the railway line where violence was not uncommon. Here, a big old house in the country, Alice was a far cry from her normal stomping grounds. For some reason she didn't like to think the wealthy people who lived in a nice place like this went go round murdering each other; that's what drunks and druggies did; but thinking about it, at least some rich people must get their money by not being very nice in the first place.

Everything was much the same as the night before, apart from the cold, with the exception of some fingerprint powder on the hard surfaces; window frames, door handles and the like. The footprints she had noticed last night before were partially gone, no doubt brushed into an evidence bag along with samples of other particulates.

Alice walked from room to room, trying to see if anything was out of place. Nothing sprang out. It was all tastefully ordered, tidy; lots of mementos and family photographs. Upstairs she looked through the other rooms before finally going into revisit the master bedroom. The sheets and other bed linen had been removed, along with the bed's mattress. Mr McKay's clothing was no longer on the floor, his shoes removed as evidence. The room was yet to be completely cleaned but the blood had been wiped away. A window had been partially opened, or was it open last night? She would have to check the photos. Nothing struck Alice as being particularly odd, well, everything was outside of her own domestic experiences, but not odder than anything she had expected.

Despite what Luca thought of her, Alice was a good policewoman. She recognised, perhaps being from such a different background was a disadvantage to her in this instance, and she was not the sort of person who was afraid to ask for help.

"Constable, what strikes you as strange here?"

"Nothing really, it's just a normal sort of house."

"There's nothing out of place, or strikes you in particular?"

"Such as?"

"I don't know. That's why I'm asking you."

Luca considered this for a second. She had asked for his opinion. He would have love to be able to point something out; prove his worth somehow. The only trouble was it just seemed to him like a pretty standard sort of place; big old-fashioned rooms (none of this open plan modern rubbish), good quality furniture (a few very nice pieces actually), some original pictures (but nothing remarkable about any of them; they were all tastefully standard Australiana), a few fine ornaments (English porcelain figurines largely), no, nothing unusual. Certainly nothing that would have looked out of place in his parent's house.

"Sorry Sarge, I don't know what we are looking for."

After a brief look around upstairs, they found themselves standing next to perhaps the house's most telling feature, the clue which the night before their inspector had missed. They were standing beside a table, and there directly above the remote control for the air conditioner, were two-family photos which had been only recently hung on the wall to cover gaps previously identified the night before as the usual position filled by a pair of small painted landscapes. It would have been telling if either Luca or Alice had spotted the clue, but as it happened it went completely unnoticed.

Alice picked up the remote control and turned the air conditioner off.

The short journey back to Wangaratta gave Alice time to talk to Luca. She was just going through the evidence again when Luca suddenly yelled out "stop the car."

"What is it?"

"The motel."

Alice looked behind them noticing the SunniSleep Motel they had just driven past. Over the years she had gone down the road dozens of times and never felt the need to stop and investigate further. Two rows of cabins arranged into an L shape with a carpark between; the once modern buildings reduced to a down-at-heel relic of the region's post war optimism.

"What about it?"

"Well," explained Luca "I just noticed as we were driving past, they have a security camera in the car park. It may give us a useful view of the road and help us establish a timeline."

A skinny girl with acne came to the door. She was wearing school uniform. Luca almost asked, "why aren't you at school?" but instead enquired about the camera.

"I'll get my mum."

Luca waited.

After a short delay the girl's mother emerged. She was wearing a facemask and asked Luca to stand further away from the door.

Luca repeated his enquiry and she informed him they weren't taking any bookings, so they didn't currently have any patrons; she was immunocompromised and had not yet been fully vaccinated. He explained he wasn't enquiring about her customers; he just wanted to see if the motel's camera was on. He discovered his hunch was largely correct, the camera was working, it was automatic and gave a good view of cars going up the road. Due to its angle however it only had a partial view of traffic on the other side of the road going to Wangaratta. What was more the system recorded directly onto her computer, so she was able to copy the cameras images onto a USB stick for him.

"That'll be $20 for the thumb drive."

Luca hesitated, it seemed overpriced, but at the same time he thought, what if it helps to catch a murderer. It has to be worth the money then. He paid up, forgetting to ask for a receipt.

Back in the car, he was just beginning to feel pleased with himself in securing the potentially valuable footage, when he suddenly realised this now meant he would have to sit through twelve hours of watching cars drive up and down the street, and here he was trying to get out of having to do all these boring jobs. In hindsight, he regretted ever saying anything and experienced a brief moment of self-pity.

Clark had always hated press conferences. It was not that he hated public speaking, it was just he hated it when there was nothing he was allowed to say, but press conferences were part of the job and in these days of instant news, it seemed they had become expected as a daily part of life. At least, thought Clark, it was better than having citizen reporters spreading rumours across social media, that could hinder his investigation.

The Wangaratta Police Station was a modern two-story brick and concrete building situated next to a park and about two kilometres from the main street. For some reason, the press conference had been arranged to take place outside the main entrance next to the car park; more Covid safe he surmised. Clark and the superintendent stood behind a podium. In turn, to their rear, were a number of uniformed officers, who although not actually involved in the case gave the impression the police were committing substantial resources to the investigation. Clark was relieved to see neither Alice or Luca were in attendance, at least someone wasn't wasting their time and actually trying to solve this case. He also knew how much Alice hated being dragged to every official event to give a "welcome to country." She had tried to explain to her superiors she wasn't a Yorta Yorta woman herself, and therefore Wangaratta wasn't her country to welcome people onto, but they seemed happy to ignore this fact as nothing more than a minor technicality, certainly nothing worth interrupting their officialised tokenism with. Beside Clark stood an Auslan sign-language interpreter. He found himself wondering if it was just in case a deaf person had happened to hear anything suspicious, and felt instantly guilty at the insensitive nature of his own subconscious.

As he liked to at press events, Superintendent Edwards took the lead.

"Good morning everybody. Sometime early yesterday afternoon a man was shot at Willow Cottage, off the Wangaratta-Yarrawonga Road. At this stage we are in a position to confirm the identity of the victim as the home owner, Mr Donald McKay, the well-known local property developer. The shooting at this stage is being investigated as suspicious. A weapon has been recovered from the scene…"

For the next five minutes the superintendent continued his report, hinting the police knew more than they did, suggesting an arrest was imminent without actually saying one was, while at the same time appealing for anyone who may have been in the area and either heard or saw anything to come forward. It was a good performance and one to reassure any casual viewer's confidence.

Clark understood the tone he was supposed to be portraying and when his turn came, he truthfully stated he had "already spoken to some people in connection to the case" and "he hoped to be in a position to make a further statement in the coming days."

After the press conference finished, he was left unsure why everyone in the media seemed so satisfied because all he had done was to give them a sound bite and a quote, neither he or his superintendent could have possibly told them anything they didn't already know.

On his way back to his office Clark took the opportunity to signal to the unfortunately named local reporter Tony Boor he'd like a private "off the record" word. Tony and Clark knew each other well from long acquaintance. Not only was Tony the Border Informer's crime correspondent, but like most local journalists he wore a variety of reporting hats, including reviewing some of June's gigs. Additionally, they were both semi-regulars at the same pub.

They arranged to meet up later in the evening at their usual haunt just out of town.

Back inside the station Teddy asked, "Clark, how's young Luca coming along?"

"I don't have a problem with him sir."

"Hardly a glowing endorsement."

Clark hesitated "The thing is I'm a bit concerned because he is an old friend of the family. Normally you'd be taking someone off the case because of that, not picking him to be part of the investigating team."

Teddy was somewhat dismissive "Oh I don't think it'll be a problem here, just keep an eye on the lad, and let me know how he shapes up."

Chapter 3 - Wednesday Afternoon

Kurt Weill and Bertolt Brecht

The Richardson case file was very slim. Ronnie Tutt had no trouble finding an old hard copy for Clark from among the massed filing cabinets in the station's archives. The file mainly consisted of the initial statements by the chief protagonists taken during the investigation; no evidence had been logged and the case had not progressed further, no charges were laid. The girl, May Richardson, claimed in her statement the figurine had been presented to her as a gift by Mr McKay but although promised he never handed it over. Instead, it had just vanished. How it had vanished had never been fully investigated instead accusations of theft had been made. In the report May didn't say why Mr McKay was giving her, his attractive young cleaner, a gift in the first place. Perhaps telling was the fact Mrs McKay had made the initial complaint against the girl and not Mr McKay himself. Clark didn't need his twenty years as a detective to see the most probable scenario here, and if, as he suspected, it was just a case of Mrs McKay trying to get rid of the younger competition then it appeared to have worked. There was no mention in the file about any threats, he would still have to chase those up, but as far as this murder case went it looked to be another dead end.

Maybe, the Richardson case told Clark something about the sort of person Mr McKay was, maybe not. Wasn't there a saying about leopards who like philanderers always remained true to character. Certainly, he really hoped he didn't have to *cherchez la femme*. Everyone he had spoken to so far about the case was *une femme*. Where was *l'homme coupable*? He'd already done enough *cherchez*'ing *femmes* for the day and it wasn't as if he believed a word any of them had told him yet anyway. Where were all honest, decent women in these days; sure, Alice was reliable, and June was, well June, but as far as the women in this case were concerned if it turned out any of them were a murderer, he wouldn't be even slightly surprised. He wanted a bit less *femme cherchez*'ing and few more facts. Less searching, more examining the evidence.

OK, Clark thought, what was the 1,2,3 of criminal detection; means, motive and opportunity.

One - Means.

Well, that at least was not hard; a shot gun. Yet to be confirmed by the PM of course but assuming he was alive when he was shot it was a gun. Of course, shotguns were always messy, no clean rifle marks on recovered bullets to match but presumably they already had the gun, although that hadn't yet been 100% confirmed. What is more, the man kept guns around the house and given the fact the gun didn't have the serial number filed off it he'd give odds of a penny to a pound the firearms register results were going to come back indicating it was his own gun which had killed him. If he was extraordinarily lucky there were prints on the gun but he didn't have much hope forensics would find any. Murderers, in Clark's experience, were rarely as obliging.

Thinking about means reminded Clark about the car. As Donald McKay's body had been found at his house, but his car hadn't been, then he must have received a lift home with someone. If he could find where his car was parked that may tell him who he had been to see, who he had gone home with and taken his clothes off for.

Two - Motive.

So far, well, he had identified loads of *femme*s, so jealousy was always a good one. There was also his money of course. When you had a victim who like Mr McKay was well off you always had to consider a financial motive. And maybe he had revenge from someone he had conned in one of his dodgy property deals. There was something funny about a couple of missing paintings too, not something that seemed like a plausible motive for a near naked dead man shot beside his own bed. No, naked was the key clue here but he wasn't going to get far with motive, not yet. Not without knowing why he had taken his clothes off. Without that vital bit of information, the motive was just going to be guess work.

And that left only…

Three - Opportunity.

As far as he knew nobody had any alibi at all and contrary to most people's intuition the lack of a good alibi rather worried him. Ask ninety percent of random people in the street where they were between the hours of x and y, and they couldn't tell you, or they would have the flakiest alibis not worth the paper they were written on, like watching the television with their spouse, someone who would more than likely be prepared to lie to protect them anyway. Murderers, in his experience, invariably had some sort of alibi prepared in advance because they knew they may need one. A really good alibi made Clark suspicious, he had even been known to bring people in for questioning based on them having too good an alibi. Nobody he had spoken to in this case so far had any sort of alibi whatsoever. If only somebody was having tea with the Chief Commissioner, then he could have made an arrest on the spot. Something just wasn't right there either.

He left his desk and went out into the reception area. Ronnie was talking to someone about people in the super market not wearing their face-masks correctly. He was being as diplomatic as possible but really, what did they expect him to do? Clark waited before he approached not wanting to get involved.

"Thanks for finding the Richardson file Ronnie."

"No trouble."

"I was wondering if you could do me another favour. Can you look up the name Sam Waters, Samuel not Samantha, through the old filing system. He would have died in a car crash about seven years ago. I can't find it on the computer."

"Even if the file itself has not been scanned and uploaded, then the old index has, so there should be a record of where it is at least."

"Well, I can't see it."

"You're probably looking in the wrong place. I'll give it a go, but if it isn't in the index properly it may take a while."

"Just see what you can do. Thanks Ronnie. Oh, and put out a call and have the lads keep their eyes open for Donald McKay's car will you."

"What's the model and rego."

"Haven't a clue, but I bet Alice has thought of it already so I'll ask her."

Back inside the general office, Alice was arranging her information onto a whiteboard; pictures of all the major participants, photos of the gun, the bed, and other details from the scene. Beside the pictures she was trying to construct a timeline, it was troublingly sparse.

Luca was on the phone and jotting down something on a notepad.

"Alice," started Clark, "Tell me about Donald's car."

"It's a Beamer, an eight series, I think. I've got the rego somewhere."

"Do we know where it is?"

"Not yet I was going to look for it later."

"Give Ronnie the specs. He can have the lads track it down for us I don't want you wasting your time on a missing vehicle. Which reminds me we should have a chat later."

"About what?"

"Not now, remind me when we're alone."

Alice looked puzzled until Clark added, "Nothing to worry about, let's just get back to the case for now. What do we know?"

"Not a lot really sir. Mr Donald McKay, shot twice in the neck in his own bedroom. Partially dressed at the time. Found by his wife. Our re-examination of the scene this morning didn't show anything new. No signs of a break in anyway. I noticed the window was open while we were there this morning but when I asked one of the forensics guys about it, he told me he had opened it to let some fresh air in after dusting it for prints. There was nothing obviously missing at the house."

"There was, actually," added Clark, "a couple of pictures. Not the sort of thing an opportunist thief could take to the local cash shop and get anything for, certainly nothing approaching their real value, but it's worth keeping them mind. Go on…"

Alice continued, "The room itself had a lot of blood but no sign of a struggle we can see. There was a weapon recovered from the scene and Luca just checked the firearms register; it was his gun. I haven't got the full forensics report yet but while I was on the phone earlier Mike, up in Wodonga forensics Mike, told me unofficially there weren't any prints on the gun, not even Mr McKay's. Not many prints on anything really. Everything keeps coming back blank."

"Except the shotgun cartridges," Luca added.

"It's not a laughing matter Constable, let's not forget to show a bit of respect, ok."

"Sorry Sarge."

Clark continued, "Good, well Mrs McKay said she left shortly after breakfast and returned early evening on her return from shopping. She has some receipts but not as many as you'd expect if she really had spent all day at the shops. Besides which, as we don't have a time of death, I'm not sure what they mean anyway. She did say she ate lunch with her husband in a café but gave nothing to substantiate it."

Alice flicked through her notes, "While we were out at the house we spoke to the neighbours. Well, some of them, most were out at work as you'd expect. We couldn't find Pete King, the farm manager, anywhere but I've left a message with his wife, Joanne. Those we did see managed to give us a couple of useful bits of information. Firstly, there was a courier van seen at the house about 2 o'clock. I haven't had time to track down the driver yet but I've got the firm, *Fast-a-wayz*, which is interesting itself. I tried the depot and they said they don't normally deliver so far out of town, apparently, it just isn't economic to go so far, so if there was a parcel drop off it wasn't on their schedule."

"So, you've got that line of enquiry covered then? Did anyone hear the gun?"

"The second thing I was coming to is someone did hear what they thought was a gun at about half two, but they didn't see anything."

"Excellent. At least we have something we can work with. Was there any useful gossip?"

"Well apparently Mr McKay had a bit of a reputation. The rumour is he had an affair which ended a couple of years ago but I haven't got a name. Someone will know, I'll try and track it down if you think it's relevant."

"We don't know yet, but given the fact he was practically naked, try your best, most men don't take their trousers off at lunchtime unless there is a reason."

Luca took up the tale, "I've just been phoning around about the business. The accountants don't want to break confidentiality of course, but off the record, admitted there is a lot of bank debt on the balance sheet. Nothing too unusual for a property developer, they tend not to use their own money if they can help it. I phoned the project manager at one of their sites, their new development over in Wodonga, and he said most of the workforce are justifiably disgruntled. It's mostly self-employed contractors not employees. Sounds as if our Donald has been a bit slow paying them. Not sure why, I guess he was just a bit of a tool. Personally, he appears to be making enough money, he just got a new car anyway, probably a lease job though. Rumour is he has been milking all the Government support packages for builders that were put in place to help the construction industry through the pandemic, only, he isn't too keen to pass it all on in a very timely manner. So, all in all, his cash flow can't be great at the moment, doing more building than selling, and he is making some people wait a very long time for their hard earned."

"Is there anyone in particular we need to look at?"

"Almost anyone in a Hi-Viz shirt and a hard hat I'd say."

"And are there any particularly dodgy deals you've heard about?"

"Well, there was something very odd which happened a short while back. He bought this particular parcel of land just on the outskirts of Wodonga, out near the Army base. Well, he paid top dollar for it, only the land was scheduled as rural so he couldn't build there. He obviously thought it was going to be re-zoned and was I'm reliably told very surprised it wasn't. Apparently, it failed some sort of environmental audit, something to do with a very rare native chickpea. Then a few months later there was a new environmental audit done and nobody could find these peas anymore. He managed to get planning permission to put forty-three units there and that's what is happening now. There is a story going around he poisoned the site to kill this pea off."

"You should get onto the local environment groups to check the story out. Try and see if there are any militant greenies who would take things into their own hands."

"I'm told there was some anti-development group camped at the site, but I haven't spoken to them yet. I've joined a Facebook group to see if there is anyone who is particularly angry."

"And?"

"They are all angry people but nothing particularly specific."

"Okay, but don't forget there is a big difference between saying you could kill someone in an anonymous social media post and actually shooting someone in the head; but I guess it's a line of enquiry for you to handle. I suggest you actually speak to someone if you can, face to face. Try the group down in the big place down by the showgrounds, I think they call themselves the GreenGuard."

"I was hoping to sit in on Sarah's interview."

"We'll see. What do you think about her skipping town, is she a flight risk?"

"I wouldn't think so. Where would she go? No, Sarah will be back in time for her evening martini."

"OK. Alice, when is your mate going to be getting the full forensics report here?"

"Well, according to Mike, there's not a lot to do really. They are checking all the blood at the scene is the victim's, and seeing if all the prints are the family's, only they forgot to get the daughter's prints yesterday, so haven't finished yet. There were also some trace fibres and particulates at the scene they are examining. Oh, and the footprint in the hall. It wasn't from Mr McKay's shoes, but they were a man's size 10's they are looking into too, trying to match a tread pattern to get a make."

"I don't suppose we can hurry them up, can we?"

"I'm doing my best, but you know Mike Owen, he likes to take his time."

"Okay, So, this is what we are going to do. I'm going over to see June about the PM results. Then I'll go over to the supermarket to speak to Mr Richardson. I'd like you to keep tracking down any of the neighbours and speak to the farm manager Pete King too. I think we need to find out who the mistress is, or was, and speak to her, particularly if she is married and there is a jealous husband thrown into the mix. Luca will cover the greenies, and you also need to finish watching the video you found and trace any visible number plates. Later we'll go and speak to a couple of the builders to see if there are any suspects there who we should be having a good look at. Luca, in particular look for anyone with a record of violence, this sort of thing is rarely done by a first-time offender. And speak to the accountants again. I want to know if he owed any money besides to the bank? And while we are looking into his finances, I'd still like to see Mr McKay's Will and discover who gets what. Maybe, Alice you can get onto that too. I'll be back later to see how you've got on. Then you two can go and see Sarah this evening if you don't mind. Alice, I'll authorise you a bit of overtime and shout you a pizza on your way home. I'd go myself but I've got to go to the doctor's."

"Everything alright sir?"

"It's just this wretched Covid vaccine, I wasn't going to bother but June keeps on about it. Have you had yours yet?"

"Had mine last week. Hurts like hell sir, the needle's about 10 cm long."

"Thanks for the image. Tom is staying at my digs again tonight so if you need me, I could be at home, but we may go over to June's place. It would serve her right if I die from a blood clot in her living room. And I almost forgot, wasn't one of you going to get me an AFP contact from the art theft unit I can speak to?"

By the time Clark finally arrived at the hospital June had completed the PM and was busy typing up her report. It had proved an interesting challenge in the end and she had earned her fee. At first glance, to the less informed or casual eye, the victim had appeared to have suffered two fatal shots in the throat, but during her examination June had proved this was not the case. The main problem, as she had suspected the night before, was while there appeared to be a lot of blood, June would in fact have expected considerably more; not that she had actually seen anyone shot in the throat before. Also there just wasn't any evidence of blood spraying, which she would have expected if his heart was still pumping at the time of being shot. The principle of parsimony led her therefore to the conclusion he was already dead when shot and had largely bled out elsewhere first. What was at the scene, while considerable, was blood leak from a large secondary wound, and not primary blood loss. June examined skin samples under the microscope and confirmed her suspicion the wound was done post mortem. So, she carefully re-examined the body. There were no other major wounds but in addition to the ragged tearing of the shotgun blast around the throat she found a small adjacent rough-cut line at one edge of the gun's entry wound. This would have been very easy to miss given the amount of post-mortem damage inflicted on the then dead Mr McKay but was quite distinct under microscopic examination. This additional wound showed he must have had his throat cut by a fairly blunt blade prior to being shot. There was also a small amount of dirt recovered from the wound so it was more likely he had been cut by some old piece of scrap metal or improvised weapon rather than a clean sharp knife. It was this cut which had been the cause of death. Evidence of post-mortem bruising also showed the body had been moved some point as it had originally been lying in a different position, probably deduced June, for about an hour.

At the start of her report June typed a succinct summary which she was in the process of reading part of this to Clark, "Mr McKay died from a rough cut to his throat by an unidentified dirty and blunt edged weapon at an unknown location. There were no signs of a struggle."

"Was he shot before or after being moved?"

"Probably after from the amount of blood at the scene. How did you know he was moved anyway?"

"His car wasn't there, so it seemed the most obvious explanation."

"So, his body was moved," continued June returning to her notes, "and shot twice in the neck post mortem at close range with a shotgun. The post mortem damage is consistent with that expected from the 12-gauge shotgun recovered at the scene."

She showed him photographs of the cut proving that he had been killed prior to being shot and started to discuss the deceased man's last meal, Nachos probably; jalapeño peppers, black beans, salsa, cheese and corn chips, when much to her surprise Clark suddenly asked her:

"If you were to get a dog, what sort of dog would you get?"

"Is this one of those silly pub games, like what superpower would you have, or who would you rather have dinner with, Adolf Hitler or Don Bradman?"

"That's easy, Bradman because Hitler was a vegetarian so I wouldn't know what to cook, and I don't speak any German either, but actually I was being serious. If you were to get a dog, what sort of dog would you get?"

"I don't know, a German shepherd I suppose, just so you couldn't speak to it. Why do you want to know?"

"Oh, just something I was wondering."

And the conversation quickly went back to a discussion of possible murder weapons, leaving June wondering if she had missed something really important.

"Let's go over it one more time."

So, June summarised her findings, going through them again for the third time, "Mr McKay died from a rough cut to his throat shortly after eating his lunch. The weapon wasn't sharp, not like a knife, and it was dirty. This had all occurred at an unknown location and his body then moved after lying somewhere else, possibly for about an hour. The shotgun wound was added later, probably to disguise the original wound."

At the end of the technical discussions about the differences in the cut marks left behind from straight, blunt and serrated blades, June, as casually as she could, asked if Clark wanted to come over and have something to eat tonight.

"That will be great," replied Clark. "Tom and I will be over around six. I'll get him to bring Genevieve and we'll be able to work on a couple of new songs together."

The GreenGuard office was in a residential part of Wangaratta but could be easily identified from the street's domestic houses as much by the piled bags of donated clothing in its driveway as the hand-made sign hanging from the iron railings bordering the street. The front room had been converted into a makeshift charity thrift store by erecting rows of trestle tables around the walls, many of which consisted of little more than old doors supported by milk crates.

The door was open and they followed the handwritten sign directing visitors to the office door at the rear of the property. Piles of boxes obstructed the walkway like the ramparts of a medieval fortification, slowing Alice and Luca's progress as they edged down the narrow corridor. Pinned to the office door was a notice informing people of how to evacuate in the event of a fire. It suggested they retreat back down the passage. They knocked.

A gruff female voice told them to "come in."

There were three people in the room, two men in their early thirties and a somewhat older woman. It was decorated with the traditional environmental paraphernalia as well as a scattering of other posters advertising a Black Lives Matter march and an 80's Rainbow Pride Disco. One wall incongruously displayed a small selection of old Shaw Brothers Kung-Fu movie posters featuring *the Five Shaolin Masters* or *the White-haired Bride from Hell.* One of the men sported a scruffy beard and had several facial piercings in his lip and nose. Despite the cold day he wore shorts and a T-shirt to show off his impressive collection of tattoos. He looked as if he had been sleeping rough, presumably because he had. Perhaps, thought Luca, on inspecting him from the perspective of his privileged upbringing, and with all its accompanying prejudices, it was because he had spent all his rent money on body art. The second man's appearance could hardly have been more dissimilar. He wore a tight-fitting grey suit with pencil thin pants and narrow lapels. His thin tie was fastened in place by an enamel CND badge functioning as a tie pin. He could have been a 1960's sharpie or the junior cashier at a suburban bank, perhaps both. Alice recognised him, and while she was surprised to see him there, she said nothing. Instead, she let the seated older woman speak first.

"And how can we help you officers?"

"I'm Sergeant Dees and this is my colleague Constable Bastoni, and you are?"

"Dedra Fernton, but you can call me Aunty De everyone does."

"Well Ms Fernton, we are asking around about a new housing development, up in Wodonga, and wondering what you know about it."

"Well, all we know it's not going ahead now because Donald McKay's dead; no loss to the World there. Hopefully someone poured the same poison down his throat he used on the plants. That would be justice, wouldn't it?"

"How do you know Mr McKay has been murdered?"

"It was on the local news, *'Prominent businessman murdered'*, it said. Prominent bastard. Your Superintendent was on the radio, apparently *'ongoing enquiries are continuing.'* Comforting to know *'ongoing enquiries'* haven't stopped I suppose. That, and the fact it isn't your job to police the correct use of the English language. So, you two are the ongoing inquisition I presume."

"And for the record, where were you Tuesday at around lunchtime?"

"We were all here, together. Well, I was up here alone and Gaz and Alfie were out the front in the stocked donation area most of the day."

"Can anyone else verify that?"

"I'm sorry officer but there was nobody here with me to verify me being alone, what with me being, well, all by myself."

"It's just routine."

"I'm sorry to hear it, to be a major suspect at my age would do wonders for the ego, but thinking about it now two of your lot came by. I didn't catch their names but they were wearing blue so you should be able to find them easily enough. Spot them in a line-up. Some complaint about running a retail business from a residential address. All nonsense as I pointed out. It's not a retail establishment, there are no prices you see. Sympathisers to our causes can take things and recycle them. Of course, if they think the items have some value we allow them to donate that money to show their support. But what we definitely don't do is fix the price of the items, the users of our service do. It's a fine line I know, but one I'm happy to walk Sergeant."

"Is there anything you can tell us about the protests at the building site. Haven't there been some clashes between you and the builders."

"Not us, dare I suggest you should do some detection Sergeant. We're a lobby group for sustainable development, nothing more. For example, why aren't all new houses made to have solar power and grey-water recycling? Why are developers not made to reserve 10% of their sites for low cost or social housing? Why do the powers that be, not mandate all new houses must have light-coloured roofs and north facing eaves to eliminate the need for air conditioners and unnecessary power use? There are lots of really simple changes anyone could make at the stroke of a pen which would make a real difference. All we need is a bit of political will and few less back handers from the construction industry into party coffers. Did you know 97% of new homes come with a built-in kitchen but only 24% of those appliances have a five or six star energy rating?"

"No, I didn't."

"Neither did I Sergeant, I just made it all up, but my point is someone should know, someone should keep track of such things. I mean why are you still even able to sell inefficient appliances? Like I said we're a lobby group officer, nothing more sinister."

"But you were camped on the site to prevent the builders gaining access, I was one of the officers who had to move you on."

"And I'm sure you did what you saw as your duty to the status quo Sergeant, but it wasn't us, they are a different group. Nice people, some of them, if a little too simplistic in their methods. We don't take direct action, we're more keyboard warriors here than actual ones. Lovers not fighters you could say. We write angry comments on Facebook pages, put up posters, maybe the odd march, an occasional egg thrown at a local councillor, nothing more."

"And the others, the ones who aren't 'nice people'?"

"The lunatic fringe. Well, I wouldn't expect any of them were actually murderers, Sergeant, for all the argy bargy they cause."

"Can you give us any names?"

"I can, I believe there was a Mr M Mouse, and a Mr D Duck."

"I seem to remember a Mr F Young."

"Well, there you are then, the suspect is already '*known to police*,' as it were. Nothing for me to add. Anything else we can help you with?"

And so, after the obligatory, "we may have to speak to you again later," Alice and Luca turned to leave the cramped office. Up until this point Alfie had stood quietly listening without adding anything himself, but as the interview finished, he stepped forward and offered to show them out.

At the front door Alfie and Alice exchanged looks.

The man glanced back up the corridor to check nobody was watching them from the office and whispered almost inaudibly, "I'll phone you."

Alice started to whisper, "what's going on Alex?" in reply, but a noise behind them told her the other man was also now coming down after them, so she stopped.

As she left, she just caught a whisper from the man she knew as Alex, but who had been calling himself Alfie, as under his breath he said a single word, "later."

Years in the police force had equipped Clark with a deep reservoir of highly skilled deduction techniques, however, none of this extensive training proved necessary in ascertaining Mr Richardson did not work 'at' the supermarket as Sarah Roberts had incorrectly claimed, rather he worked 'for' the supermarket. A simple phone call to the manager had revealed this much and more. He also discovered Mr Richardson was employed to drive a delivery truck. A quick check had told the manager he was currently half way back from his normal delivery run to their warehouse near Geelong, as he would have been at a similar time early afternoon the day before hand, and on the day before, and the day before that too.

Clark decided to go and see his wife instead.

The Richardson house was only a few minutes from the McKay's house located on the far side of the McKay's farm. It had originally been erected shortly after the second world war as a short-term seasonal residence for fruit pickers; the Richardson's had been living there for over twenty years. There was a small array of rusty farm equipment outside much of which dated from the same period as the buildings themselves. The home itself was of basic fibre sheet and corrugated roofing tin construction, a cheap and functional method favoured by previous generations grateful at just having their own four walls and not insisting on having a parents' retreat, multiple living areas and three en-suite bathrooms, or even a bedroom per child. It gave the impression of being held together loosely by its peeling paintwork; signalling, by its dilapidated condition, the long-term neglect from both landlord and tenant.

Mrs Richardson greeted Clark like an old friend in an affable somewhat motherly manner and showed him inside. The house smelled of tobacco smoke and vapour rub; the television was on, it never occurred to her to turn it off. There was one living area, lounge furniture at one end and a kitchen table at the other. She offered him a coffee, and as the kettle boiled, she commenced his enquiries for him by stating, "I expect you've come about Donald."

Mrs Richardson, Clark estimated, would have been in her late forties although her hard leathery skin could have easily belonged to a much older woman; her face creased like a semi-deflated balloon. She wore a flannelette work shirt over a simple pair of working pants, and no make-up. Her hair was greying but still maintained hints of its original flame red colour.

"Did you know Mr McKay well then?"

"Well, I did, years ago you understand."

"Am I right in thinking Mr McKay was a bit of a ladies' man?"

"Like I said it's all a long time ago, been married nearly twenty years now, long time ago."

"And there has been some sort of falling out, between the two families?"

"Well Inspector, we was never round their house for tea or nothin' but I always got on fine with Donnie. Liked his first wife too, back when she was alive. Knew 'er as a girl before they wed you know. Now she was a lady, like something off the tele she were."

"What can you tell me about his current marriage."

"I wouldn't be the one to know. Don't see 'em."

"So how did this rift start? There was some sort of statue involved I understand."

"Well Donnie gave our girl it, a sort of thank you or something. He was like that Donnie, one day he'd quibble over a few cents in ya' pay packet, the next he'd spring you a slab of beer round as a thank you. Anywho, his new wife, she sees it missin' and all hell breaks loose."

"Well why do you think he didn't just clear up the misunderstanding?"

"My thoughts is if he told his wife why he had given our May the bloody thing his wife would have really given him hell for it. It was easier for 'im to just not say anythin'. You know our May weren't ever prosecuted or nothin'. Donald saw her right and made sure there weren't no charges."

"So, out of curiosity, and it's not my case or anything I'm going to follow up on you understand, does your daughter still have the statue?"

"Well as a matter of fact she don't, gave it to me she did. It was really for me all the time see." She took a large sip from her coffee as if no further explanation was needed before adding, " 'old on a minute I'll show you it."

She got up and briefly left the room. When she returned it was with not one but two small porcelain figures, one a shepherd with a sheep and his sheepdog and the other of a shepherdess holding a lamb. They were a bit cheesy for modern tastes but obviously antique, finely made and well painted.

"The two of them are a pair see. Donnie knew 'cause he'd give me the first one about twenty years ago. I recon when May reminded him she'd seen one a bit like his, he remembered and sort of wanted to get the shepherd and the shepherdess together again."

"You don't think he was sending you a message, he wanted to get together with you, his shepherdess, again after all these years?"

"Never thought of it, don't sound like Donnie tho', too, what's the word?"

"Cryptic," suggested Clark.

"Yeah, all too cryptic. I just thought it was more that things like this are worth more in pairs, like. They are, aren't they?"

"I understand so, yes."

"I means, wot a cow of a wife thinking my May would sleep with her husband just for a bit of old tat like some cheap tart."

Clark resisted the urge to say, "well you did," and instead he thanked her for all her help. He saw himself out.

Outside she asked him, "you're not say nothin' 'bout the statue will you?"

"I don't think its pertinent," replied Clark before adding as a clarification a simple, "no."

As he was leaving, she said regretfully, "I'm sorry about Donnie, he were a bit of a sod at times, but there weren't no real harm in 'im."

After seeing Mrs Richardson Clark went to get his vaccination. He wished he could go and interview Sarah Roberts instead but knew June would nag him if he missed another appointment. Despite June's accusation he wasn't vaccine hesitant, just very busy. He consoled himself with the knowledge Alice would be able to fill him in later, and decided he'd better just go there and get it done now and stop putting it off.

The vaccination appointment had of course gone smoothly and without any delays, which was a good thing because on his way home from the doctors Clark had arranged to see an old friend, the Border Informer's crime correspondent, Tony Boor. As was their usual practice they met on neutral ground, the pub.

Tony was a seasoned reporter having worked in newsrooms for nearly forty years. A career which had taken him to a major metropolitan paper until, after marrying, he had returned to his roots and a job at the local Informer group. There were few jobs at the paper he hadn't held, including a short spell as editor, but his real love was local politics. His 'who to vote for' opinion pieces on election day were legendary and his endorsement was still much sought after, even in these days of reduced newspaper circulation and social media influencers.

The pub Clark and Tony chose to frequent was quiet without being gentrified, a throw-back to old fashioned hospitality and simple décor; a row of solid looking dark bar stools sat in front of a hammered brass counter, a sideboard displayed vintage memorabilia.

Clark ordered the drinks, "two pots please, the Beechworth pale ale. On second thoughts, better make mine an orange juice."

"Feeling alright Clark?"

"I've just had the bloody injection and June says I'm not supposed to drink for a couple of days."

After paying the barmaid the two took their drinks outside into the beer garden where they could enjoy the peaceful evening air beneath the dappled shade of the birch trees.

Clark began, "You've been following rural politics for ages Tony, What's the story on old Joe Bastoni?"

"As in the Victorian minister for gaming and liquor licencing. Mr Regulation himself?"

"Yes, that's him?"

"I thought you were investigating the McKay murder."

"Well," said Clark "I am."

"Am I allowed to know how Joe Bastoni is connected to the murder, off the record."

"Old friend of the family I'm led to believe, nothing more."

"Sorry, I'm not really in that loop anymore. Gippsland's a bit out of my turf these days."

"But in the old days?"

"Well, in the old days, the rumour was Joe had some very unsavoury connections, the Garci Brothers and that vicious little racketeer Sonny Fabrini."

"Any truth?"

"I doubt it, someone trying to wog smear him by associating his name with a couple of known underworld figures of Italian heritage."

"By his friends shall ye know him," misquoted Clark.

"In politics sometimes, well, let's just say sometimes it's useful to shout 'fire!' even when there isn't any smoke."

"So rural politics at its racist best?"

"That's about it. Not sure where it all started now, it may have been the anti-regulation mob trying to smear him because he wanted to restrict the number of pokies machines, or more likely the right wing of his own party, get his de-selected."

"But you think he's clean?"

"Pollies all cross the line sometimes. Not that there is much of a line these days. I'd say he's as clean as any of them but you don't get to be in cabinet by being St Francis of Assisi; not in his party anyway. A bit of a hypocrite but par for the course."

"In what way?"

"When he was young, he was a bit of a playboy racer. Now he's all about family values."

"This is just background stuff I'm after and all off the record you understand."

"Clark, I gave up on trying to get a big scoop thirty years ago."

"Thanks Tony, you've been very helpful. Let me get you another of those."

"I don't mind if you do. Did you know they had a son?"

"Yes Luca, I know him, he's in the force."

"No not Joe Bastoni, The McKay's, Donald and Lizzie, they had a boy too, Angus I think, something Scottish anyway."

"You said had."

"He died, quite a few years back. I think it ended the marriage indirectly. Some families are just filled with tragedy it seems."

"And others," misquoted Clark again, "have tragedy thrust upon them."

> *Everything must have an end*
> *So the poets say*
> *Our romance like all the rest*
> *Will end some sorry day*
>
> Raymond Klages and Billy Fazioli.

It was an almost unvarying routine. After breakfast, and before work, Sarah and Colin Waters would take their dog for a walk in the park; an onlead only walk that lasted fewer than twenty-five minutes. Often it was the only time in the day the two of them had together uninterrupted by televisions, telephones or teleconferences. For many people walking the dog in the morning was something of a chore, something to get through before starting the real business of the day. In the Waters' household however, dog walking was a special part of the day, a time they fiercely reserved as a couple. As they walked, they never appeared in a rush; never hurrying towards its finish, while at the same time never exceeding their schedule.

This morning as they entered the park one at a time through the bright green kissing gate, they were greeted by someone they both knew. Standing in a sweaty t-shirt and track pants beside a bouncing German shepherd puppy, obviously with more energy left than its exhausted looking owner, was Luca Bastoni. Private couple time or not, there is very little you can do when you see an old friend with a new puppy other than stop to say hello.

Luca greeted Colin with a loud exhalation of his name as if totally surprised to see him there, "Colin!" and proceeded to kiss Sarah on the cheek, adding, "I'm so sorry to hear about your stepfather."

"Mother said you had called yesterday, twice. I was a little later home last night than I expected I'm afraid."

"And I'm sure either I or my Sergeant will have to call again later. This is Ella by the way, not mine yet I'm sort of borrowing her, a sort of trial run. So far, I'm doing all the running, I don't think she has broken a sweat."

"She's lovely Luca."

"And seeing we are doing dog introductions, who is this?"

"This is Mr. Sandman, he's eight."

Luca bent forward and patted the more subdued Labrador's offered neck.

"Good morning, Mr. Sandman."

"You're local then Luca?" asked Colin.

"I'm just around the corner."

"I didn't realise police pay was so good."

"I'm sharing a rental, It's OK for now. I'd love my own place sometime of course."

"Look Luca," said Sarah with just the slightest hint of exasperation in her voice, "what do you want to ask me?"

"Like I said, I'm really just walking the dog before work, but if you want to talk now of course I can. I mean it's all a formality really, isn't it."

"I've already spoken to your boss you know."

"Well, alright then. We'll leave it for later. Why don't you and Colin come down the station this afternoon and we'll do the formalities while I take your fingerprints."

As a solicitor Colin was familiar with his rights. "You'll need a warrant."

"It's just for elimination purposes, like I said it's all just standard procedure. I mean I'm sure we could get a warrant if we had to but I rather hoped you would want to cooperate."

"No," said Sarah, "of course we'll cooperate. So, there were fingerprints found at Donald's house then?"

"I really am not allowed to comment, but off the record, yes. But that's one old friend and dog walker to another, you understand. Of course, it doesn't mean they are the murderer's, does it? They could be your mum's for all we know at this stage. Which is why we need to eliminate those of the family. I really shouldn't be telling you any of this. I mean, I'll tell you when I can."

"Thank you, and of course we'll both come down to the police station later today Luca."

"That would be good. In the meantime, there is a rather delicate matter I'd rather I investigate myself, you know, quietly as a family friend, rather than with all the police siren's flashing."

"Which is?"

"Who was your stepfather having an affair with? I know he was, because he always was, I'd really just like the latest name. If it isn't connected to the investigation nothing will become public, you have my word. We've known each other long enough for you to know what my word's worth."

"The thing is mother doesn't know, and I'd rather she didn't."

Luca decided to have a guess. "Was it Mrs Richardson, May's mother?"

"God no, I think he did once, but I'm sure that was over long before he and mother married. You know he tried it on with May though? Anyway, what gave you that idea?"

"I don't know. I spoke to her on the phone and I just got an impression, something about how she spoke of him, there was real regret in her voice. So, if it wasn't her, who was it?"

"And you promise you won't say anything?"

"I said if you tell me and it isn't relevant, nobody will need to know, not my Inspector, not your mother, nobody. But, if my Inspector finds out, and believe me he is a very capable man and will unless I can promise to him he doesn't need to, well, his lack of diplomacy is common knowledge. I just need a name."

"You promise Luca?"

"You have my word. A name."

"It's Aunt Jeannie, my mother's sister."

Constable Luca Bastoni did not own a dog. He did not want to own a dog. Renting in a share house it would have been almost impossible for him to own a dog. This didn't bother Luca; he was not even sure if he really liked dogs. If asked, Luca would have admitted he was more of a cat person; not that he personally owned a cat, Luca hadn't even been able to keep the potted plant he had received as a flat warming present alive, and it had been a cactus; it was just cats were agreeably independent, and a neighbour was always happy to pop in and feed the cat if you went away for the weekend. Dogs, in Luca's opinion were just too hard logistically to be worth the effort.

Luca normally kept his uniform at work. His routine involved running to work and showering and changing there. It was a habit he was happy to forgo, happy to be out of uniform if only for a short secondment. Today, knowing Sarah and Colin owned a dog, and having from time to time seen them out walking it in the morning, he had borrowed Ella to make it easier to have a casual chat. It had been a while since he had even spoken face to face with Sarah and he didn't want their reacquaintance to be a formal interrogation. Luca, was ambitious, he needed to get something to help his career by personally assisting in this case, and to do so meant making sure he was an integral part of the whole investigation. Borrowing a dog, was a small ploy, but one which had appeared to have worked. He had the name he was after, even if not the name he had expected. Only now he had two problems, firstly, how could he possibly keep his word to Sarah given the whole point of the exercise was to prove to Inspector Reynolds how indispensable he was, those two objectives seemed incompatible. His second problem was somewhat more straightforward, what could he do with Ella for the rest of the day.

At the station Luca brushed a few stray dog hairs off his trousers, dog hairs didn't blend unobtrusively with his dark blue pants. Initially he tried tying Ella's lead onto the leg of his desk and placed a bowl of water next to her. She promptly spilled it over the floor. Just tying her lead up for the day wasn't going to work.

He untied her and walked her over to Inspector Reynold's office.

"Good morning, Inspector. I've just got to run this dog back to the Tommo in the dog unit. One of the police dogs had puppies a few weeks ago and I borrowed this one earlier only, I can't keep her here. He said he had a few potential buyers later, so I'd better run her back. I'll only be a few minutes."

Clark came round his desk, looked down at the playful young German Shepard, and gave her a pat. "What's her name?"

"Ella."

"Hello Ella, are you named after Ella Fitzgerald? Good girl. Good dog."

Turning to Luca, he continued "Aren't police dogs all neutered?"

"I wouldn't know sir."

"Well, there are a few things we need to do this morning. First, we're going to head off and see an old friend, Frank Young." He thought for a second before adding impulsively, "just bring the dog."

Francis "Frank" Young lived in an old school house with a small group of fanatical followers. If they had followed a spiritual calling, he would have been described as their cult leader. As it was, they simply called themselves, 'the Commune.' The school house itself, or ex-school house, was one of many similar buildings scattered around the state which stood forlorn and abandoned due to the steady inexorable decline in rural school enrolments. Frank and his commune had not acquired the buildings in any conventional sense, instead one day they had simply occupied them and despite the best efforts of the authorities continued to do so. The Education Department were at a loss. It had been suggested they sell off the site to divest themselves of the problem. This strategy, given the presence of its current occupants, had up to this point been unsuccessful. Whatever success they had evicting the group had only been short lived, at best only lasting a few days before the unwanted residents simply returned by breaking back in. In the end they had decided a solution to the problem was too hard and resigned themselves to ignoring it.

Frank had two wives and a seemingly innumerable hoard of children. Not that either of the women concerned took the title, "wife" of course, instead labelling themselves as, "companions" for legal reasons. Over the years companions had gone and been replaced, but the commune endured. This core group over time had been joined by a handful of other fellow commune members, each with their own colourful stories and complex menagerie of relationships. On the night of the last national census there had been a total of fifteen adults and twenty-two children at the site and their most common religion had been listed as New Earth Jediism.

Periodically, Frank and his group had adopted a number of causes, the environment being only one in the long list. Whenever there was a protest, Frank was there. He had marched in support of indigenous groups, striking workers, at queer pride rallies, and to show his support for the legalisation of cannabis; this last cause being the one campaign particularly near to his heart. Whenever there was something to demonstrate against, Frank would find a way to be involved.

Given his history, it would have been surprising if Inspector Clark Reynolds and Francis Young's paths had not crossed before, and of course in a rural area like the City of Wangaratta, no such surprise was forthcoming.

Clark, Luca and Ella found him, as usual surrounded by his associates, on the old school cricket field. He was down on his knees, trowel in hand, beside a bucket of potatoes.

"Good morning Francis, bit late for spuds, you should have harvested those weeks ago."

"Not an offence is it Inspector? I see it's not just policemen who are getting younger," said Frank, pointing at Ella, "police dogs are too."

"Don't mind Ella, she's just helping us with our enquiries."

"Speaking of which?"

"Can we have a word privately, let's have a stroll."

Frank stood up and brushed the soil off his knees. His clothing hung awkwardly off his slender frame as if it resented the shape of its current occupant, an objection it had not had towards its previous owner.

Frank motioned to the others he was okay, as he and the two police officers set off together; Ella bouncing along beside them, excited like any other puppy would have been by the abundant attention of so many small children.

"Your name has cropped up in our enquiries concerning Donald McKay, the former chairman and chief executive of Willow Property Developments."

"Yes, I know of him. Former, you said."

"He was murdered early Tuesday afternoon, you didn't know?"

"What I do know is it wasn't me, Inspector. I was here on Tuesday in the garden and have the broad beans to prove it. Not much of an alibi I'm afraid, but I didn't know at the time I would need one."

Luca, was still determined to make a favourable impression on his boss, something he was unable to do by just quietly listening. He had a sudden hunch and decided to act on it.

"I understand you knew his wife, Emma."

"I don't know where you heard that, we've met of course but I wouldn't say we knew one another."

Having gone this far Luca decided to try again with a second equally wild guess.

"I suppose Jeannie introduced you."

"Correct, I met her through Jeannie, but I have never met Donald."

Clark continued.

"You never saw him at one of your anti-development protests?"

"I see a lot of people I don't know who they are Inspector. Lucky for you I'm not in the habit of murdering them all."

Luca felt a little annoyed his inspector had dismissed his line of questioning so quickly and decided he'd try again, "And how do you know Jeannie?"

"We've been on a few sit-ins together. She's a fellow environmentalist, as I expect you know."

"She's not one of your groupies, is she?"

"Careful officer, your bourgeois middle-class morals are showing at the edges. I'd watch that if I was you, before someone starts believing you aren't serving the whole community, just the right-wing petty-minded Fascists."

"I mean…"

"I know what you mean Constable, we are acquainted but not biblically. If there are no other questions about my intimate relationships, I've got some potatoes to attend to."

"And what is your relationship with Emma McKay."

"I told you, we've met. End of story."

"So, you and her …erm…aren't…"

"Bridge partners, mortal enemies, lovers?" Frank turned to Clark, "your Constable's got a one-track mind Inspector."

After they had concluded their chat with Frank, and were in the ute on the way back to the station, Clark asked, "what did you make of him?"

"Not sure sir."

"Well, I think there was something he was trying to tell us."

"He was?"

"Maybe not trying, so much as, not sure if he should tell us. He wouldn't give a direct no when you asked him about Emma and her sister would he? So, tell me about Jeannie."

"It's a private family matter sir, I'm not sure of its relevance."

"Why don't you just tell me and then I can tell you if I think it is."

Luca's objections lasted for a while as they drove back to the station but as soon as Clark had warned him withholding evidence from his senior officer was not going to help his career, he finally gave in.

"I don't want this to go any further, I gave my word to Sarah, but I'm confident her Aunty Jeannie was having an affair with Donald McKay. We know he was the type, don't we? So, I asked Sarah this morning if he was having an affair with anybody these days and she said in confidence he was, with Jeannie, and believe me she'd know. According to Sarah, he was until recently. I think she may still have been. Now if Emma McKay or maybe Jeanie was also seeing Frank, it leaves us with a potential mess of people all cheating on each other. Maybe Frank was trying to use blackmail to stop the development and it got out of hand. Somewhere I think one of them fits into the puzzle, only I told Sarah I'd speak to her Aunt first, and only tell you if there was no other way."

"And how long have you known about all this?"

Luca feared he had blown his chance, he may have to wait years for another decent murder, years to get another chance to push his career forward because now there would be a mark against his name. How could he get the inspector back on his side now? All he could do was tell the truth and hope for the best.

"Jeannie, I only found out about this morning, I wanted to tell you but the only reason I didn't is because I promised I wouldn't."

"And, what about the connection between Jeannie and Frank Young."

"We still don't know anything for sure do we? It was just a complete guess."

"Normally Constable, I'd have you reprimanded and kicked off the case at this point. By rights you shouldn't have been part of this investigation at all knowing the victim, but today is your lucky day and I'm going to give you a chance."

"So, I can speak to Jeannie?"

"No, I am going to see her. You can stay at the station doing paperwork and I'll let you off without a formal file reprimand, just this once. Never, ever, do it again. If you know something you tell me at once. Is that clear enough for you Constable? If not, you can spend the rest of your career supervising a school crossing for all I care, you sure as hell won't be one of my detectives."

While they had been out of the station, Alice had discovered what she obviously thought was an astonishing piece of information. On their arrival back in the office she was waiting to greet them with this new revelation. She had spent the last couple of hours at Mr McKay's solicitors going through his Last Will and Testament, and although some of it was as expected, it did contain a few potentially useful insights. The bulk of the estate, such as the house itself, had unsurprisingly been left to his widow, along with most of a not insubstantial share portfolio, including half of his business. Of the remaining items, a quarter of the business had gone to his stepdaughter Sarah Roberts, while in the next paragraphs, he had outlined a series of minor bequests to distant relatives as well as some to people from his business dealings over the years; small items to assuage his guilty conscience. It was not until the end of the Will when Mr McKay dropped, what to Alice seemed something of a parting bombshell.

Alice opened her copy of the will and read allowed the closing few lines, "and I leave the remaining 25% of my shares in Willow Property Developments to my sister-in-law, Mrs Jean Jones, while I leave my favourite two impressionist paintings; *The Willows* by Fredrick McCubbin and *Dandenong Summer Day* by Charles Condor, to my only daughter, Miss May Richardson, who admires them so much, together with the sum of $100,000."

As surprising as she found the will, she was equally astonished when neither her inspector nor the young constable seemed in any way shocked by this news.

Instead, Clark just said, "yes but did Jeanie kill him, I don't see the motive, and how would she or May could have known what the will said anyway?"

And Luca added matter-of-factly, "She's not a big woman so I can't see her being able to move the body alone."

"The same is true of Emma McKay, isn't it?" observed Clark

"So did the sisters do it together because of May Richardson?" speculated the young constable, happy to still be allowed to contribute after his dressing down in the car earlier.

Clark considered for a moment, "I'm not sure of a possible scenario here, but my money is at least one of those three is involved; the jealous wife, the mistress-in-law or the illegitimate daughter. I just can't get a handle on which one yet. I'd be a whole lot happier if we had identified the actual murder site; I think it'll all fall into place then."

Alice wasn't slow catching on. "We haven't really looked have we. How are we going to discover where he was killed?"

And so, the conjecture continued going round and round in circles. Clark could feel they were close now, the truth was near, buzzing just out of reach like a particularly annoying melody line from a song you heard on the radio and knew, even though you didn't like it, you would be humming for the rest of the day.

After a few minutes Clark decided, "Okay, I'm going to take Ella home, Tom's still there and he can look after her. Give me the forensic reports. I'll see if anything stands out. Alice, Luca, let's tie up all the loose ends. I suppose someone should go over to see May Richardson herself. We need to establish if she even knew Donald was her biological father, let's just leave that one until I get back so I can speak to her myself. I have a hunch it isn't relevant but let's make doubly sure. Before then I want you to do some research, try and get valuations for those antiques and paintings in the will. At the least find out what they were insured for. Oh, and one more thing, I'm still not happy about our old friend Frankie Young. Ask around, has he ever been seen at the McKay or Jones houses, you know the sort of thing, go through the files and read up about his involvement in the protests. Can we link him, or any of the other protesters, directly to Donald McKay. When you've done, I want you to pick me up from my house and we'll go and see this sister. While we speak to her Luca is going to stay here and wait for Sarah and Colin to come in to give their statements, and one last thing, did you ask the solicitor if anyone actually knew what was in the will?"

"He said not, but Donald had a copy so I suppose someone could have found it. I forgot to tell you need to talk to Alex Bunning at some point sir."

"Isn't he on some undercover operation for the organised crime unit?"

"We bumped into him at the Greenie's place. He said he'd call, but hasn't."

"I'm sure he will, when he can. I'll speak to the Super to find out what he is working on, but the last thing he needs is for us to go blowing his cover. Not in a case when one person has been killed already."

Pirouetting towards Luca Clark continued, "Okay then Luca, you start by looking into the paintings, I'm sure they will be separately insured. Also don't forget about the art theft unit in Canberra I was talking about. I was going to speak to someone myself but I think I'll let you do it, they may be able to help you. There isn't anyone local I know of who could fence a picture like those, I don't even know if you could even sell them. I don't like coincidences, and these pictures going missing at the same time as his death just doesn't sit right with me. And when you've done that, Luca I think you've still got several hours of motel video footage to watch."

"Alice, if I can have a word in private."

When the two were alone Clark asked, "so what do you think of our young Constable Bastoni?"

"Bit full of himself sir; thinks he's Sherlock Holmes."

"Not much of a team player you think?"

"Keen to make an impression though isn't he. Has he done anything in particular I should know about?"

"Let's just say I'd be happier if you'd take him under your wing for a bit. Show him the ropes. I get the feeling from the Super we're going to get stuck with him for a while and we can do without him flying around like a loose cannon."

"Don't worry, sir, I'll keep an eye on him."

After she left, Clark picked up his files, grabbed Ella's lead and strode out the office. He wondered if he was doing the right thing, handing responsibility for Luca off to Alice. He was a bright lad, and may even make a decent enough detective once he knew how the system worked, but there was a system; the Super was his boss, he was Alice's boss, and Alice was the constable's boss. That's how the police service worked. It was true, as Alice had said they were a team, but they were also a hierarchy at the same time. The sooner Luca discovered it and stopped expecting special privileges because of his family connections the sooner he'd become a useful officer. It was just a shame he had to get Alice to explain it to him, but it was exactly the system he needed to learn.

While Tom was taking Ella for a quick walk Clark sat at his table, a sandwich and the forensic report in-front of him. He was so engrossed he didn't notice Tom had returned and was looking over his shoulder.

"They're cool pictures. Can I have copies for my science class?"

"It's a murder Tom. I can't really do that."

"The microscope shots I mean, not the ones of the dead body. I love all that geology stuff. I could put it in my Crystals and Minerals unit for the year 9's."

Clark looked at the microscope images. He hadn't really paid them any attention. The label said "S6; Hall Floor; x-pol ft 5X10." The imaged looked like something from a child's kaleidoscope; rounded shapes with rainbow-coloured edges, pretty but not particularly informative.

"First Tom, can you tell me what's so good about these pictures, what do they show?"

"One of the way's you can identify mineral samples is under a microscope," explained Tom in full teacher mode. "Normally you can't see much at all, but when you have a black light or the right sort of microscope filters, you can often tell what sort of mineral you are looking at from the colours you get, and as a result maybe even where it came from."

"And these images?"

"See here, these pictures say *S6; Hall Floor, x-pol ft 5X10* I assume that's the technician's shorthand for sample six, taken from the hall floor, examined under crossed polarised filters at fifty times magnification, or a five times eye piece and a 10 times objective lens."

"So then," asked Clark, "what mineral are these?"

"It doesn't say how thick the sample is so I can't tell precisely how much the light has been refracted. What I can say however is this: the grains are rounded and all of a very similar size. If I had to hazard a guess, I'd say they were a graded washed sand."

"Which still means nothing to me."

"I suppose it could always be from a beach but up this way it's more likely to be builder's sand."

"Okay, I'll bite, tell me about sand. Only let's pretend I'm not in your year 9 geology class."

"*Sand* is a very general term." explained Tom trying hard to not sound like he was giving a lecture. "What we really mean is one of a group of silicate minerals, minerals made of largely silicon dioxide."

"You mean quartz."

"Possibly, largely, but sand is really just broken bits of rock and can contain feldspars too. Now while they are largely silicon and oxygen compounds, they also contain other elements. These are in the sand sometimes just as impurities, normally as metallic ions. For example, there are silicates containing sodium, and others with potassium and aluminium. There are loads of them."

"And which mineral is this?"

"I've said, from this photo I can't tell you, but I can tell you this, if I had the original sample, and some samples from various quarries to compare it to I bet I could tell you which one it came from."

"He was a property developer, so I'm not sure knowing there was builder's sand in his hall will be helpful at all. Builders probably all buy the stuff from the same one or two companies anyway… but didn't I see somewhere …"

He flicked through the report further until he came to the line reading, "*There were no yet identified particulates other than carpet fibres recovered from the victim's shoes.*"

Glancing through the report again he found hardly any fibres were identified on Mr McKay's clothing, it was as if they had all just been washed.

Thumbing through all the pictures Clark found a second microscopic image, this time of the fibres retrieved from Mr McKay's shoes.

"Tom, what do you make of this one?"

"It's some sort of nylon carpet isn't it, all straight uniform tubes." He checked the scale. "It would be a very short pile carpet though, wouldn't it? What are they from a car boot?"

Chapter 5 - Thursday Afternoon

Sam Theard

It was late in the afternoon when Alice and Luca approached their inspector's front door. On the right of the entrance was a doorbell with three buttons arranged vertically; only one was marked, 'ground - C. Reynolds.' Alice pressed it and the intercom emitted a sharp buzzing sound, like a startled wasp.

June answered explaining, "Clark's gone to bed, he's a bit off colour after his Covid shot."

"Sorry," apologised Alice, "we can come back."

"I'm sure he's alright really, just a mild case of man flu. I'll see if he's asleep. Just come in for a minute, don't wait out there."

June buzzed the door open and they quietly entered through the narrow hallway where there were a variety of old Jazz posters on the wall and went on into the front room.

As bachelor pad's go, Clark's apartment was fairly typical; comfortable, masculine. He had surrounded himself with his favourite things; CD's, old records and books, many of which had overflowed from the available shelving and formed piles on the floor. Most of the records were Blues or Jazz, but there were plenty of others as well, reflecting an eclectic taste. In one corner of the room an old washstand was currently functioning as a well-stocked drinks cabinet. There was not a single cushion or floral throw rug to be seen. The remaining furniture; leather sofa, glass coffee table and a pair of lounge chairs, was all finely-made and functional enough, but it had not so much been arranged as shoved into a mismatched interior patchwork up one end of the room in the alcove formed by the room's bay window. A tall standard lamp gave off a harsh glow, illuminating an open book and a whiskey tumbler on an occasional table. The far end was Clark's music set up, a personal studio for his keyboard and guitar, in addition to his amplifiers and a small mixing desk. A connecting doorway had been widened to open onto a kitchen area. There was no dining table but bar stools and dirty plates showed Clark was in the habit of sitting at the kitchenette's breakfast bar to eat.

After a couple of minutes Clark emerged, he looked a touch the worse for wear.

"Evening Alice, Constable, how did you get on?"

"Well firstly, I managed to get onto *Fast-a-wayz*, the courier people. It turns out the van driver had a special arrangement with Mr McKay. He does a few private deliveries from a wine dealer; Mr McKay paid him on the side, not much, just enough to make it worth his while to do the extra drive out from town. He dropped off a case on Tuesday but didn't see anyone. He said, he left it in the shade next to the front door. Apparently, there is nothing new in that."

"He saw nothing then?"

"He says not I'm afraid."

"Could he confirm a time?"

"Not precisely, but his official deliveries are all time recorded by the computer when people sign for them. The previous one was at ten past two and the next wasn't until quarter past three; so, he had about an hour window right there. Looking at his route I'd say he must have been there nearer half past than two o'clock."

"So" said Luca, "he would have had time and opportunity himself."

"But, as far as we know no motive," pointed out Alice. "However, if he was there then it's likely the murderer wasn't because he would have seen them. He said nobody was home, he knocked."

"I don't know," mused Clark, "how long does it take to drop off a box of wine? I don't think we are any further forward here."

Luca asked, "What do you want us to do about the driver?"

"What about the driver?"

"If he is being paid on the side," clarified Luca. "Isn't that conspiring to defraud the tax office sir?"

"But we're not the revenue collectors Luca, and we don't even know for a fact he isn't declaring it as income anyway. Let's not waste our time trying to chase the tax on twenty bucks on behalf of the ATO and focus on catching a murderer shall we. Tell me about the Richardson girl. Have you contacted her yet?"

"It didn't take long to track her down, she's only over in Beechworth, and she'll be at work this evening. We were just coming to pick you up because you said you wanted to speak to her yourself. I thought we could all go over there now. She seemed very upset over the phone."

"Can you go Alice; I'm not feeling up to much right now. By the way has Alex Bunning been in touch?"

"He's coming in first thing tomorrow morning."

"Hopefully I'll be in and we'll see him together."

Clark turned to address the young policeman, "Now Constable, what happened when Sarah and her husband came in, have you got everything we need?"

"Actually, they were a no-show sir. I thought perhaps I'd go and chase them up."

"I think they'll wait; I'll do it myself. You go with Alicet to see Miss Richardson. Let her take the lead though. Watch, and you may just learn something. We'll catch up again in the morning."

Chapter 6 - Thursday Evening

Gene Austin and Roy Bergere

Luca was quiet in the car all the way to Beechworth. Why couldn't the inspector see he was quite capable of interviewing a few people by himself? How was he supposed to get his chance to impress if he was stuck being the sarge's errand boy? He considered going to see the superintendent about it. "Teddy" had assigned him in the first place, and he knew dad from way back. Maybe he would have a word on his behalf. Tonight, he'd just have to put up being treated like a kid he supposed, he didn't like it though. Perhaps if it was a different sergeant it would not be so bad, but Alice, well, everyone knew she had only been promoted because she was indigenous, what was he going to learn hanging around with her?

It was dark when they arrived at the Beechworth Asylum. In the car park, loitering next to a minibus, they found a young man in a "haunted Beechworth" t-shirt. His sickly pale skin giving the impression he was a ghost himself; caught, like a deer, in the car's headlights. Alice wondered if it was intentional. On being asked he immediately informed Alice and Luca, May Richardson was currently giving a party a guided tour and would be about an hour. He recommended they wait in the café, but instead Alice decided to go inside and catch the tourists up. Most of the passages were dark, but up ahead there was a light illuminating a small group of visitors huddled around a doorway. Their guide, May, was inside.

"This room was the last one used by Beechworth's final inmate, one of the small group of patients still here in the 1990's," announced May Richardson. Her assembled tour group peered through the door as if they may still get to glimpse a man in a straitjacket tied to his bed if they tried hard enough. "This room has not been changed since then, except the bed sheets, which were washed last Thursday." It was a poor joke, but delivered with good timing, and they dutifully laughed. Changing her tone she continued with her rehearsed script, "The ghost of one of those final patients, who died when being given electric shock treatment, still walks this corridor regularly. I've seen him, and if you're really unlucky you may see him tonight yourselves. He's not a happy chap, believe me, we don't want to run into him. He has been known to throw things at people." There were a number of dissenting murmurs from those who obviously felt the presence of an angry poltergeist would only enhance the tour experience. May went on, "if you all follow me, you'll be able to see the electric treatment room where he died, in agony, strapped to a chair while hundreds of volts were shot into him. All done to make him feel better of course. Then I'll show you one of the earlier cells used in the 1880's. It's in the old North Wing corridor and is now the home to one of our other ghosts, the famous White Nurse. She mysteriously died here in 1902, the day before she was due to be married. Her death was never explained but perhaps not co-incidentally her fiancée was hung for killing a Yackandandah woman two years later."

After the tour May Richardson and the two police officers sat in the café. It was closed, but May went behind the counter and poured the remnants of a coffee jug into three mugs. She didn't bother heating it, clearly she wasn't expecting them to stay long.

"So," started Alice. "How well did you know Mr McKay?"

"I've seen him about since I was a girl, up at the house. I've really only known him to speak to though for a couple of years. I knows Sarah better really, I used to help out with her horses."

"So, are you saying you didn't know him very well."

"Not really, we used to talk sometimes while I was cleaning his office. Just normal stuff, and we discussed some of his paintings and the bits and pieces in his house. He had some nice things, and he used to show them t' me, the pictures and stuff."

"Did you ever discuss the small paintings in the hallway?"

"The one of the house you mean? Yes, he was very proud of that one."

"What can you tell us about why you were sacked?"

"I left."

"Some misunderstanding about a figurine of a shepherd."

"Well, he just saw me one day admiring this little statue, and I said something like how my mum had got one a bit like it, and he says I should have it then, so I had one too. Says I should think of it as a thank you for all my hard work. When his wife started up, he asked me not to say anything and he'd take care of it and make sure I wasn't charged or anything, just he didn't want his wife to know he'd given it to me. All this nonsense, well it's his wife really, not Mr Mc or my parents."

"There were threats?"

"Well dads got a bit of a temper at times but he didn't mean anything by it, just talk like."

"I'm sorry I must ask, what exactly was your relationship with him?"

"I wasn't sleeping with him if that's what you're thinking."

"Honestly, it's the very last thing we thought."

"Well, you tell his wife. I'm sure that's what she thinks. A case of the pot calling the kettle if you ask me."

"When did you last see him."

"Not since then."

"Has he been in contact?"

"About a week ago he phones me, asked if he can come round for a chat like, but he never did."

"Any clue about what he wanted to discuss?"

"He didn't say."

"So" continued Alice trying hard to be as tactful as possible, "and believe me there is no easy way of asking this question, and this may come as something of a shock, did you know your mother and Donald Richardson had an affair."

" 'course, they didn't, just his sour cow of a wife again I expect. Putting out stories. You should take no notice of her. Like I said, she shouldn't throw stones."

"Anyone in particular you know of?"

"No one I can say, but I knows."

"Just one more thing, for the record, where were you on Tuesday between say one and four in the afternoon?"

"I was at College all day."

"Really," interposed Luca "what are you studying?"

"Why, you think I'm too thick or something?"

"No, I asked so I can check you were there."

"Well as it happens, I'm training to become a nurse. I spent the day learning about patient handling, you know, transferring beds and in the shower, that sort of thing."

"And your course is at Wangaratta?"

"No, I go up to Wodonga."

"Isn't it a bit far to go."

"Not really, it's not every week, most of it is remote access learning these days you know, so I do most of it all at home. I only have to actually go in about once a month."

"And coincidently was this Tuesday?"

"Yes."

"What time were you there?"

"All day."

"And your tutor can verify you being there?"

"Yes, I expect so, we had to sign in because of Covid. You can check the register if you like."

After the discussion Luca and Alice walked back to the car.

"So, Luca," started Alice, "what did we learn?"

"She's a bit defensive."

"That's just because she didn't like you. What else?"

"She didn't do it."

"Because?"

"She has an alibi we can check."

Alice continued, "and what else?"

"I don't know, Beechworth is haunted by some sort of dead nurse?"

"Well, I was thinking more about her not knowing our victim was her father myself."

"Do we? She could be just a good actress, but I guess it's unlikely."

"Good, we're agreed then. I'll let you report to the Inspector in the morning."

Luca looked at her, not sure what else to say, eventually he came up with, "er, thank you Sarge."

Alice acknowledged him by asking, "now, where shall I drop you?"

> *Oh, Sinnerman, where you gonna run to?*
> *Sinnerman, where you gonna run to?*
> *Where you gonna run to?*
> *All along dem day*
>
> Les Baxter and Will Holt

Clark woke to the noise of rain beating against his roof, settling the dust and increasing the humidity for the day. He felt a slight pang of guilt about hating the rain, how often had he been told about it being good for the farmers? He knew it was true of course; he did a bit of gardening himself; just a few veggies, nothing like June's beautiful garden. He tried to turn over only to discover Ella was still asleep on his feet. June was standing over him with his breakfast on a tray.

"Are you feeling better now?"

"A bit thanks."

He accepted the tray, thanking her again adding, "you needn't have stayed last night, I must have been particularly poor company."

All June said in reply was, "Are you well enough to get up now?"

"I have to be really, don't I?"

"You're either well or you aren't. If you aren't, stay home. Medically speaking if it was a bad vaccine reaction, which seems likely, it's not a bad idea to get up."

The coffee and subsequent hot shower revived him some more, and by the time he was dressed Clark felt almost ready to progress with his day.

In the kitchen Tom was waiting for him at the breakfast bar, as always, his beloved double-bass was within reach. It looked almost as if he and Genevieve had been sharing a piece of toast.

"I reckon I'll push off this morning."

Clark told him, "You know you can stay longer if you like?"

Tom appreciated the offer but as much as he enjoyed the company of his friends, after a few days, Tom found himself needing his own private space; an artistic solitude he was only willing to share with his creative partner, Genevieve.

He made his excuses, "I know, but I'd better be off, things to do. Anyway, you know the rule about house guests and fish," before adding, "and there's a train in about an hour. June has offered to run me to the station when she comes back."

The two of them sat there as a man on the radio droned on about how much the latest lockdown had hurt his profits, how Coronavirus itself hadn't damaged his business it was the Government's constant shutting down and opening up that had.

"But," said Tom, talking to the radio, "how much is a person's life worth?"

Tom swore uncharacteristically angered by what he obviously felt was the man's crass comments.

"I put a bloke away once who killed people for about $250," Clark told him.

"I'd like to think that's not all a fellow human's life amounts to."

"I don't think the murderer's life amounted to much."

"So, some people, say Mozart or Einstein, are worth more than others?"

Clark was semireligious. He went to church fairly regularly but wasn't always sure it was for the right reasons. Sometimes he felt it was more to listen to the choir or hear the organ blasting out a great piece by Bach; but if it was the music that fed his soul who had inspired the music? Either way he didn't feel anyone's life wasn't of value and regretted his previous flippant comment.

"I'm just saying…. I mean, I'm sure hospitals make decisions like that every day. Do we spend out finances on this ultrasound machine or three more beds in the surgical ward? What's the best bang for our medical bucks?"

Clark was just about to add, "and speaking of doctor's where's June gone anyway?" when the door opened, and in walked June and Ella, sodden from the rain. June hung her wet umbrella at the door and kicked off Clark's now muddy old Blundstone boots.

"I'm going to borrow your ute to take Tom to the station."

"But I need my car," pleaded Clark.

"Tom and Genevieve won't both fit in mine. If you're going to work you can take my Audi. We'll swap tonight at my house." And with a quick kiss, and a hand over of keys, she and Tom had gone leaving Clark in a kitchen rapidly taking on the distinct aroma of a wet dog.

He unplugged his phone from the charger next to the toaster and called the office. As he expected Alice was already at work.

"Morning Sergeant, I'm just about to leave my house, I'll meet you over at Willow Property's office in about half an hour."

"Do you want me to bring Luca?"

"No, get him to do something useful there, where he won't get in the way."

By the time Clark arrived at the carpark the rain was already stopping, for all the damp inconvenience there had only been a couple of millimetres in the gauges and the road was already drying. Alice greeted him.

"Morning, Sir. Lost your dog?" she joked.

"I've had to leave her at home, didn't want to risk June's upholstery. What happened last night with May Richardson."

"Well, I told Luca he could report to you on our meeting, but basically I don't think it's anything to do with her. So, why are we here specifically?"

"I've been thinking. Up to now we've been working backwards in this case. We found a body and tried to go back to when he was alive. I think it's time to work forwards and see if that approach gets us anywhere. We know he left the house early on Tuesday morning to come here. Let's see what happened next and try to go forwards."

Inside the offices they showed their identification to the receptionist and were ushered to see Mr McKay's personal assistant, Sandra, in the meeting room.

The meeting room had stood empty since the start of the week; the coffee had all been drunk, the biscuits had all been eaten. At one end of a long table stood an easel displaying an artist's impression, a row of neat new houses interspaced with perfectly manicured identical crepe myrtle trees; a developer's idealised dream of suburbia. On the table itself was a model of the pictured development, complete with a scaled down row of miniature figures roaming the streets like toy soldiers on parade. In the model driveways stood gleaming tiny cars, perfectly maintained without a dent, respray or bald tyre between them. Beside the model was a stack of spiral bound brochures proudly proclaiming the proposed site to be called "MyrtleVale."

The two police officers introduced themselves and asked about the previous Tuesday.

"Well, it was a big day," explained Sandra. "Mr Mc had a meeting with the bank and it didn't go too well. Afterwards he was in a foul mood."

"Do you know what exactly happened."

"Well, he was just going on about how you'd have thought they hadn't even heard of the Covid-19, and how there couldn't be a single project in the whole world running on time for twelve months. Of course, we're all used to the boss's tirades, sometimes they could last for hours."

"So," deduced Clark, "the business was in trouble?"

"Not really, it's not like they demanded their money back. They knew they couldn't get it anyway. And they didn't really say no to this new project either, it's just they wanted the old development to be a bit further along first. They said we were being spread too thin."

"Do you know if there was something else bothering Mr McKay; something to explain why he was in a bad mood?"

"I don't think so, he just thought it was really stupid of them because we've already purchased all the land and have already got all the planning approvals sorted out. He was just saying it was all as much their problem as it is ours, only they're all too thick to see it."

"The bank saying no was unusual?"

"Very, but what with Covid I guess everyone's cashflow's gone to pot and the bank won't be in a position to say yes to everyone, whatever their ads say."

"So, Mr McKay's mood could have just been about the bank and the Wodonga delays?"

The assistant considered this suggestion for a moment before replying.

"The whole project's been a disaster from start to finish. First, we thought we had all the planning tied up. We had all the little council ducks lined up one by one, until one of them turned around and shat on us. Donald was most pissed. He used to say *in the old days you could take a man's handshake to the bank*." She said the last bit in her best Donald McKay voice only remembering part way through her boss was dead. Sandra paused sniffling and wiping her eyes, hoping that they hadn't noticed, before saying, "I'm sorry I haven't offered you a coffee."

"That's alright thank you."

Sandra buzzed the intercom and spoke to the receptionist. She ordered herself a drink, double checked to see if either of the police officers had changed their mind, and continued.

"Well, after all the planning seemed to be sorted, we had the fiasco with the rare native plant people. That held things up too, until Mr McKay paid someone to resurvey the site and discovered they weren't there. And then we couldn't work on the site because there was too much smoke from bushfires, and finally, when we got it all started, we had Covid of course."

"Do you know who Mr McKay was dealing with about the site survey or the planning permission?"

"I could look it up later if you like, but not off the top of my head, no. He used to do things like that himself,"

"Back to Tuesday. What happened after seeing the bank people?"

"Let me check." Sandra flipped open a large one-page-per-day A4 diary. "The bank meeting was supposed to be finished up about ten but ran over, maybe quarter past. Afterwards Mr Mc was going to have a brief Zoom meeting with the architects but there was something wrong with the connection and they ended up rescheduling. That maybe all took a quarter of an hour at tops. I'd say he left to go to the Wodonga site with Luke somewhere between half ten and eleven."

"And who is he?"

"Luke Isleworth is a consultant project manager. He has worked for Mr Mc before, mainly when people need a good kick up the arse. Mr Mc was going to sack Nico, the current site manager, and appoint Luke instead to get the project back on schedule."

"Do you remember at what time they left the office?"

"Somewhere between eleven thirty and twelve. He was due back in the afternoon for a four o'clock with someone from the council about an access road, but he didn't show. I left a message on his phone but he didn't get back to me."

"Was it common, he'd not call back?"

"It wasn't unusual, sometimes he would disappear for an hour or so but he normally phoned in afterwards. I just thought his phone didn't have any reception and he didn't realise. At half five I went home expecting him to just turn up Wednesday morning as usual."

"So, where could we find this Luke Isleworth?"

"As far as I know he's at the site today. I'd start there. Hang on I'll get you his number if you'd like."

Shortly thereafter, Clark and Alice left the offices of Willow Property Development to continue retracing Mr McKay's movements through his final day hoping to find out which had been his last and most disastrous of appointments.

Wherever you go in Australia building sites always look more or less the same. There are always larger-than-life trucks, men in Hi-Viz vests, partially constructed buildings with their exposed framework resembling the rib cage of some long extinct species of colossus, and of course dirt, gigantic piles of dirt. Typically, you will find a fence around the whole area protecting the assorted equipment and building materials from any unauthorised people, although contrarily, there are some who will tell you the fence is really an attempt to protect the people from the assorted equipment and building materials. These people generally claim it is something to do with occupational health and safety. The site will, to satisfy those people, invariably proclaim proudly it is a hard hat area, sometimes with an additional sign compelling people to drive at an impractically slow speed that would result in your vehicle being overtaken by a passing asthmatic snail. In these respects, Willow Developments' site on the outskirts of Wodonga was a site much like any other. If anything marked it as being particularly different to the hundreds of other sites up and down the country, then it remained unnoticed by Clark and Alice as they turned off the highway and through the site gates.

On the way there, Clark had ignored June's original instruction. Instead, he had dropped her little sportscar off outside the hospital, so when he and Alice arrived, they were in Clark's more robust ute. He drove straight up to what was unmistakably the site office. The sounds of two men arguing could be heard from inside.

Clark told Alice to, "ask around a bit," and then entered the portable cabin by himself.

One of the men turned and barked a, "what do you want," type of challenge.

Unfazed Clark introduced himself, holding up his police identity for verification.

"I suppose you're here about Don McKay."

For a builder, the man speaking was unexpectedly well dressed, an attempted look spoilt somewhat by gum boots and mud on his rolled-up shirtsleeve. The second man wore the more traditional tradies work outfit; Hard Yakka and Hi-Viz.

"Yes, and I expect full cooperation with our enquiries." Clark didn't need to add a threat, one was implied by his commanding tone. "You are Mr Isleworth?"

"That's correct," he replied, before backing down somewhat and adding a conciliatory, "and of course how can I help?"

The man in the work clothing stormed out leaving Clark and Luke Isleworth alone in the small on-site hut.

"Let's start with what can you tell me about events last Tuesday morning."

"Well Don phoned me at the end of last week about problems he'd been having here. On Tuesday, he and I had a meeting in his office about a different project, one up at Albury. Now a couple of those houses have been sold off the plan but not really enough in terms of the deposits paid to do any work. Don wanted some interim financing options because cash flow here has dried up; too many of the houses started but nothing finished; and there are no part payments coming in because someone's stuffed up all the scheduling. We were trying to convince the bank to be a bit more flexible."

"And it all went badly I understand."

"Well, it could have been better, so now we just have a bit more pressure to get this site rolling along again; try and get a few finished so we can get a bit of cash in rather than having loads part built and no income."

"And you then came here?"

"No, we tried to have a meeting with Don's architect online first and then I came here. Don nipped off to grab some lunch, it was probably eleven or twelvish guess. He was going to meet me here."

"Are you saying he never arrived?"

"He phoned, said he was going to see someone and would be late, told me I'd have to sort it out."

"And what time was that."

"I don't know."

"Can you check your phone log for me please."

Luke Isleworth fiddled with his phone, scrolling through his incoming call records.

"Here it is 12:03."

"Did he say where he was going, or who he needed to see?"

"Sorry, no."

"What happened then?"

"It was all a bit awkward actually, he made me hand over my phone to Nico, that's Nico Sandros the old site manager, and he sacked him, then and there over the phone. Nico was furious, threw my phone out the window, swore all sorts of threats. I thought he was going to hit me but he just stormed off."

"Any threats against Mr McKay?"

"Against everyone, 'he'd hunt him down,' 'make him pay,' that sort of thing. The bastard even smashed my car headlight with a shovel when he was leaving."

"Did you report this?"

"Not worth it really, I mean I'll just put it on expenses so what's the point? I mean I'm not going to claim the insurance to fix something that costs less than the excess am I?"

"It wasn't Nico you were arguing with when I arrived?"

"No, and that was nothing anyway."

"It didn't sound like nothing."

"Inspector, a couple of the houses were supposed to be glazed and watertight by yesterday only there were some delays. I told them if they couldn't get it finished, they had to make sure they got everything covered with plastic because it was going to rain overnight. But someone didn't do his job so now I've got a bill for water damage I shouldn't have. So, no Inspector, I'm not happy, but it's nothing to do with Donald McKay."

"And you are sure Mr McKay didn't arrive here at any point later in the day."

"He may have I suppose, but I never saw him, not after the meeting in his office with the architect."

"Okay. Now what can you tell me about this site. Why is it so behind schedule? What do you know about native plants and the planning permission?"

"First, Inspector, as far as I know there are no rare vulnerable or threatened plants, and there never have been. Those photographs sent to the council are of the stony bush-pea, and if anybody at the planning department had any brains at all they'd know that it grows only on rocky hillsides so it wouldn't be at our flat housing site anyway. I'm reliably told by Mr Google the nearest location where that species grows is over 100 kilometres away. If there were some here then they aren't indigenous to the site and someone put them here to stop us building. I suspect however it's just a photo taken somewhere else for the same reason. It didn't work because an environmental site survey proved there was nothing here. It may have caused a small delay, but overall, it was not serious."

"So, why is the site so behind schedule then?"

"Covid-19 mainly. Half our workforce live in Victoria and half are from New South Wales. When the border closed, we lost a couple of weeks work while everyone sorted out the whole border bubble travel arrangements. Then the supply of materials, many of which come from Melbourne, dried up. I'd feel kind of sorry for Nico really if he hadn't smashed my car. Not really in his control. He even had to shut the site down a few days last summer before Covid hit you know, because of too much smoke."

"And how do the tradies feel now, there doesn't seem to be very many about?"

"Well, they aren't happy, but we've given them some incentives and some back pay and it's starting to get back on track now."

Clark made him go through the story a second time before leaving. It was a habit he had gotten into when he was unsure about something, but the retelling of the tale was virtually the same, with no major inconsistencies.

Outside Alice was chatting to a couple of the builders. Clark walked over, but while on the way over, he noticed a pile of sand. He stopped and placed a small sample into an evidence bag.

Once in the car Alice briefed Clark on what the builders had told her. They largely corroborated Luke Isleworth's story; none had seen Donald McKay on Tuesday and they also confirmed there had been an enormous row between the two site managers, Nico and Luke Isleworth.

"So where does this leave us then boss?" asked Alice.

"I don't know yet. If Donald McKay hadn't been to the site," reasoned Clark, "but builder's sand was found in his hallway, it's likely a builder must have visited him."

"This Nico Sandros person."

"Could be," confirmed Clark, "he's certainly joined my list of suspects."

"I'll track him down then and we'll go and have a word."

As Clark drove quickly down the highway Alice phoned Luca and asked him to look up Nico Sandros, just to see if he had a record.

"Most sacked employees don't turn around and murder their old boss," she told him.

"Agreed. So, it's likely to be the motive, but let's get Luca to check out this Isleworth bloke too."

Even as she spoke to Luca, she found herself wondering, if Nico was involved why was Donald McKay undressed when they found him. Still, Clark was right, it's always better to check on these things anyway.

Luca could be heard tapping his keyboard.

"I've found a Nicholaus Santos, 32, lives locally in Yackandandah, a couple of minor incidents, oh, and he also glassed someone in a pub fight, so obviously got a bit of a temper. He did a couple of years for that back in 2016. Nothing since."

"That sounds like our boy, put it on my desk and I'll go through it with you later, we're off to see an old friend first." A formality really, another of those loose ends needing to be tied up, but that was how cases were solved, following all the possible threads to their conclusion; it was that 99% of methodical perspiration that got the results and not the inspector's spontaneous flashes of inspiration; most of the time anyway.

Turning off the road near Wangaratta they drove for a further ten minutes towards Milawa.

The Milawa dairy café was a favourite haunt of June and Clark; it was just far enough out of town to make it unlikely they would bump into anyone Clark knew professionally, or who wanted a quick consult from June, but not so far it took a long drive to get there. It had good food too. Important considerations for them because to most people both the local police inspector and doctor were always on duty. Today Clark was at the café with Alice having a coffee, when to all appearances they did just happen to bump into an old acquaintance, Alex Bunning.

Alex sat down and ordered a coffee, exchanging pleasantries while the waitress bought it over. Cup in hand he got straight to business.

"As you know I'm working on a case undercover. My unit is investigating criminal corruption in the building industry and we are looking at a number of residential property developers."

"So, what's the link to the environmental groups?"

"Over the last few years there have been a string of incidents at proposed building sites. Most involve some kind of dispute over planning permission. Now the one you are concerned about, as I understand it, involved Willow Property and a rare native pea. Now while it appears to be just a clumsy ploy to have the development stopped, maybe by the environmentalists, we believe, well suspect actually, because of the pattern, it's someone at the state planning office trying to get their share as a pay-off. They plant the evidence, if you pardon the pun, and then tip off the environmentalists, who, not realising it's a set up then cause a stink. The idea is for a price some corrupt guy in the planning department then offers to smooth it all out."

"So, you are trying to find them by seeing who is tipping off the environmentalists?"

"Exactly, well, initially the plan anyway. What happened here is even more interesting. The builder's problem went away very quickly after your boy, Donald McKay, instead of paying off the planer decided on an alternative strategy; he hired Stevie Dunn as a consultant instead."

"And who is Stevie Dunn exactly?"

"Well, Stevie is a bit fixer for hire with all sorts of criminal links. There are two options we are looking into; Stevie paid someone off, presumably the person in the planning department, on Donald's behalf. Not impossible, but it would be out of character. The second, and more likely one in our view, is Stevie lent very hard, on whoever they are, and pocketed the cash for himself."

"So, you are now posing as an environmentalist but really looking to the corruption in the planning office and to see if they have had any contact with this Stevie Dunn."

"That's about it. We have a lot of intel regarding some sort of connection between Dedra Fernton's environmental group and the planning department but we don't know the exact relationship. It was the GreenGuard, for example, who were first at blowing the whistle about these bush-peas. If anybody passed them the information directly, we'd love to know who. So, I'm currently trying to find out and get evidence against them. Other agents are looking into it from inside the council offices to see if they can identify the person being bribed or threatened. Of course, ultimately, if we can pin anything on Stevie Dunn's associates, would be a massive bonus. If we could get something big on him, we may be able to do a deal and make a real dent in the Melbourne underworld."

"What sort of organised crime are we talking about exactly?"

"All the usual rackets, but Stevie isn't really picky. Drugs mainly, ice, but he's mixed up in the Maverick Motorcycle Gang, and they do a bit of everything."

"So, do you know how Donald McKay knows a bikie fixer like Stevie Dunn?"

"At this stage, no. But Stevie's the type who has a way of getting himself known, and it wouldn't be the first time a known criminal has had some connection to property development."

"What do you know of the murder?"

"Well, there has been some talk of course. Nobody seems to have liked Donald McKay much, not the environmentalists or his employees anyway, but nobody is bragging about it or hinting they know more than the rest of us. Unless he promised to pay Stevie Dunn for fixing his problems, and was stupid enough not to, I doubt Stevie's involved. Bikies don't generally kill civilians. Occasionally maybe to send a message but not normally, you don't get paid by dead people."

"So, are you staying undercover now he is dead?"

"I'm going to stay on a bit to see if the change in management at Willow Property could lead to some developments. Stevie may try to make himself known to Donald McKay's widow. That's our hope now, he'll want some sort of pay off we can trace."

"Have you looked into his company's finances?"

"The story is they are in trouble. Have been for 18 months. Covid hasn't helped of course, and then there were all the delays on the Wodonga project. I've heard on the grapevine they are trying to get another project up and running and the bank is losing patience with them and said no."

"We've heard similar," Alice informed him.

"Well," said the undercover officer, "we had a girl posing as a temp in their accounts department. She was trying to find any payments or receipts which didn't make sense. She didn't get far before we pulled her out, she didn't uncover any obvious pay-offs anyway, but she reported the broad outline. It doesn't look too good."

They continued their conversation and coffees for a while but learnt nothing new. Constable Alex Bunning agreed to inform them if he heard anything about the murder, and they agreed to steer clear of the undercover organised crime unit's investigation to protect his cover.

They left separately.

Luca's morning had not exactly been the thrilling game of discovery he had hoped when the superintendent had first told him he was going to give him a short secondment to the detective branch. He should be out there interviewing suspects, not scrolling through hours of motel carpark camera footage looking for, well, he wasn't even completely sure what he was looking for. He had hoped when the phone had rung the inspector had something more interesting for him to do, but instead it was the sergeant asking him to look up a suspect just to see if he had a criminal record. How could he prove his worth stuck in here doing dead end tasks like that? Still, the sergeant had given him a long list of jobs to do, boring jobs anyone would have to admit, but he'd do them anyway. He just hoped once he had proved he was a team player he would be able to do something a little less tedious.

The first task she had asked him to do was to get Donald McKay's mobile phone out of evidence and look through the call log. The phone itself had been locked of course but his secretary had told him the password, 1,2,3,4, so it hadn't been a problem. The last call he had made was to Luke Isleworth at 1:47. He had two incoming calls recorded afterwards, both his secretary, both listed as missed calls. Unfortunately, he couldn't get any location data off the phone. Maybe the spies at ASIO could but not a police constable in Wangaretta. He would have to ask the sergeant he supposed, maybe she knew a way.

Secondly, she'd told him check the traffic camera up at the traffic lights. If Donald had left his office at midday on Tuesday, then he should be seen driving past it on his way to the Hume highway about a quarter of an hour later. That had drawn a blank because, as he discovered, it only takes pictures of cars going through the red light; Donald could have driven past it all day for all the use it was. He suspected the sergeant had known it was a long shot at best. But, he thought to himself, if Donald had been driving that route, he would have had to go down the high street, and through the roadworks. Luca decided on a long shot of his own and had a phone round of the shops. It had been worth the effort as he had discovered the jewellers had a camera in the window and they hadn't recorded over Tuesday's file. He'd go and pick it up and have a look, he may be able to see Donald's car drive past. He'd also stop at the roadworks and see if there was a traffic camera there, thinking about it he was sure he had seen a sign telling drivers there was.

The third job on Alice's long list was to check to see if the café at the arts centre had a record of when Mr McKay and his wife shared his last meal. Well, they should, thought Luca, people have to sign in when they visit a business these days because of the Covid pandemic. Since Donald McKay had eaten lunch, nachos, if he recalled correctly from the autopsy report, he could get the time off the cafés Covid contact tracing registers. All he'd have to do was phone the Health Department and see if their contact tracing QR code system could help him. At the very least he should be able to ask if the staff remembered serving him.

Leaving the station, now, he thought to himself, this is more like it. Time to be a detective.

On a fine day the penthouse of the Rockz Orlando Hotel offered a magnificent view over Sydney Harbour and was one of the jewels in the crown for the Orlando Hotel Group. That morning however, the panorama went almost unnoticed by Marion Westlake. She was so used to living in such luxurious surroundings if anything she considered staying in the $12,000 per night suite as slumming it. After spending 14 days of Covid-19 hotel quarantine in the suite if she felt anything at all waking to views of the harbour bridge and opera house it was ennui.

Today, Marion had a full diary, and while she disguised her ferocious work ethic with a thin façade of easy-going charm, she was not a hands-off heiress as many had come to realise too late. As vice chairman of her family's hotel chain, she took the business of enhancing her considerable fortune seriously and her close staff knew of her ruthlessness only too well.

Marian did however have one indulgence, a love of paintings. She was a well-known collector of mid and late 19th century art, and had often claimed, when interviewed by glossy society magazines, her love of art stemmed from a portrait of her great-great grandmother by Whistler. This was only partially true; her family did indeed own the famous Whistler but it had been removed to a bank vault in Zurich before her birth and she had never seen it hung. Instead, it was more likely her art appreciation came from an episode with an art student in her early twenties the family had assiduously managed to keep out of the tabloid press.

Her artistic passions had recently turned to early Australian Impressionism and at a recent auction at Sotheby's Marion had managed to acquire two pictures by Arthur Streeton and a sketchbook by Tom Roberts. She had been actively looking to add to these and when a small gallery owner in Melbourne had contacted her about a pair of landscapes by Charles Condor and Frederick McCubbin, she had become almost uncharacteristically excited and arranged for the him to bring the pictures to her for a private viewing. Unbeknown to the gallery owner she had invited a Dr David Boothby, Professor of Art History from the University of Sydney and leading expert on the Heidelberg school to assist her in her appraisal.

And so, from her vantage point perched overlooking Sydney harbour, the representatives of three quarters of the art world met to discuss the two pictures: the collector; heiress Marion Westlake, the critic and expert; professor Dr Boothby and the dealer; gallery owner Denning Mathews. The only omission would have been an artist to explain or defend their work, but in this case, neither artist was available, or, indeed needed. The artistic merit of either picture was never considered. No mention was made of line, colour or composition, let alone whether either picture was in any way attractive, other than if it confirmed the identity of the supposed artist or not. Denning quickly perceived that Ms Westlake had no interest in art, per se, and all she could she when looking at a picture was a big dollar sign. It was a pity, he thought, art lovers were much easier people to deal with than soulless investors. Denning may have been a bit of a scoundrel, a rogue even according to some, but at least he had occasionally let his heart rule his head; detached a pictures worth from its price tag.

The meeting had lasted only a few minutes. Following her expert's advice Marion had quickly passed on the supposed cottage by McCubbin but had asked if she and Dr Boothby could borrow the other painting, purportedly to be by Charles Condor, in order to perform a full appraisal on it. Denning Mathews had refused; there had been no sale. Marion had even refused to reimburse Denning for his expenses.

After the meeting Marion Westlake was annoyed, annoyed and disappointed. She wasn't the sort of person to take having her time wasted lightly. And so, feeling particularly spiteful she asked her secretary to phone the Australian Federal Polices Art Crimes Unit in Canberra and informed them of the existence of at least one Heidelberg school forgery which was currently on the market.

When Clark and Alice arrived at the McKay home for another look around, the door was unlocked, and there was an unknown car parked outside which neither of the detectives recognised. There was something still bugging Clark about the place since his first visit on Tuesday evening and he was determined to get to the bottom of it.

Inside they found a squat lady vacuuming the house.

Clark and Alice introduced themselves and informed the cleaner she was not supposed to be there as the house was still being investigated as a crime scene.

Her reply displayed no connected logic.

"But I always come on a Friday."

"I'm sorry but you can't clean today, Mrs ?"

"Mrs Armstrong."

"Hopefully we'll be finished soon and you can come back then."

Mrs Armstrong seemed unconvinced, "but I do the old peoples home Mondays, Wednesdays and Saturdays, and I do the Centre and Kinder' on a Tuesday and Thursday, and the library too, after they shut of an evening. I only have Friday's here."

"Well, I'm sorry you can't clean today. Can you show us what you've already done please?"

Mrs Armstrong admitted she had only just started, having up to that point cleaned the upstairs bathrooms and toilet.

"So you weren't here last Tuesday?"

"I've told you haven't I? I'm only here on Fridays."

Alice picked up the conversation with the more standard question; "How long have you worked for the McKay's?"

"Don't know to be sure. About twenty or twenty-five years I'd say. Maybe more."

"Oh, I thought May Richardson used to be the cleaner a few years ago."

"Put it this way I've never saw her holdin' no mop. May have hung around in the study some, helped with a bit of filing, but she never did no cleanin'."

"So the McKay's are good people to work for? I mean if you've been here so long."

"Old Donald, I mean Donald what you're 'ere abouts father. Now he was a real gent. And Donald's mother. I liked her."

"But Mr McKay?"

"You don't say ill about them what's dead I was taught."

Alice persisted, "But you didn't like him?"

"He weren't one to get in my way, that's all I'll say."

"And the current Mrs McKay?"

"Well current's about the size of it. I gave 'em five year when they married and five years it been. Recon there'd have been another Mrs McKay before too long."

"It wasn't a happy marriage then."

"Bound to end in tears sometime. All their business I guess, I just clean the house."

"Before you go." Clark paused to give her time to process she would have to leave as requested. "Before you go, I've a couple of things you can help me with. Can you please show me where Mr McKay kept his wine, and his guns."

She led him to the rear of the house where the laundry was situated next to the kitchen. In the laundry there was a door leading to a cellar under the house.

Clark lifted the latch and went in. There were racks of wine bottles neatly arranged in groupings by type such as Shiraz, Pinot Gris, Chardonnay. There were also a few fine bottles on display.

"And you haven't cleaned down here?"

"I hardly never come down here, no reason to."

"Thank you have been very informative, and the gun case?"

"In the study."

She led Alice and Clark back up the narrow stairs to the ground floor. The study was exactly what Clark had expected, leather chairs arranged next to a small coffee table and the whole room dominated by a large desk. Against one wall was a row of filing cabinets with a door between.

"It's in there."

Clark opened the door finding inside a private cloakroom containing a toilet, a sink and pressed into a far corner an old yellow metal locker currently functioning as a firearms safe. Clark tried the gun case's door but it was locked.

"Do you have a key Mrs Armstrong?"

"No, I don't"

"So, you haven't touched inside."

"Not without a key I ain't."

"Thank you for your help. My Sergeant will let you know when we've finished, if you could go with her now and give her your details on your way out."

After she had gone Alice asked Clark why he wanted to see the wine cellar and the gun case.

"You remember on the day in question there was a delivery of wine," explained Clark. "Well, where is the box? When I got here it wasn't at the front door. There are no odd boxes in the cellar left unpacked. None in the recycling. Mrs

McKay doesn't strike me as the type who would carry a case of wine to the cellar and put it away at the best of times, certainly not if she had just discovered her husband had been shot and was waiting for the police to arrive. It's all a bit odd isn't it. Another piece of the puzzle to solve."

"And the gun case."

"Well, I wanted to see if it was still locked. Who steals a gun, or anything else come to that, and locks the box afterwards? The only person to lock a gun case is the gun owner, or maybe someone else in the household. I don't remember anything about it in the forensics report. As it's locked, was it even fingerprinted, inside or out? Do the forensics boys have a key? It's something we need to check up on."

"I'll phone Luca and get him to double check the report now if you like."

"No. I think you should phone Mike up at forensics directly, he may have done it but just not put it in his report because there was nothing there to report on."

"So, is that what has been worrying you about the house?"

"Not really but one thing has occurred to me, everything's too clean."

"Well, they do have a cleaner."

"No, I mean where is the blood? The victim was shot at close range but there is no blood other than the bed. We know, he was shot on the bed, but June says he was stabbed first and then carried upstairs. So why isn't there any blood on the stairs or the carpet in here. His clothes were on the floor but as I recall there was no blood on them either. Again, it doesn't add up."

"But isn't it just because he had already bled out?"

"I don't think so. My guess is that even if he was murdered somewhere else and then brought here and shot again to cover up the first wound, just like June said, then there would have been blood on his shirt, and maybe some drips on the floor, somewhere. The killer carefully cleaned up all the blood because it didn't fit their, 'shot on the bed' story before leaving. It's like they were setting a scene for us to find. Trying to make us think he was killed by a jilted lover."

"Doesn't that imply they knew that they wouldn't be disturbed?"

"Exactly, which brings us back to Mrs McKay's involvement. She was shopping, we are told. If true how did the killer know she was going to be out long enough?"

"And there is the matter of the missing pictures," added Alice.

"Go on," encouraged Clark.

"Well, he had a copy of his will, so it's very likely she had access to it too. If she was a jealous wife, it is also likely she would be spiteful enough to not want his illegitimate daughter to inherit them."

They considered the possibilities.

"But" Alice began, "I still don't understand why the clean shirt."

"Because she was afraid there was something on the old shirt, something other than blood from his neck wound to link him to her as his killer. She was just covering her tracks."

"So, what we need to do is find his real clothes, the ones he was wearing when he was killed? Could she have burnt them? Is there an incinerator on the grounds?"

"I don't know," answered Clark, "but I think now you mention it that's what has been bugging me for days. This house was all wrong; it was hot on Tuesday so why was it even hotter indoors, and they had the air-conditioner on in the hall. The reason was someone had lit the wood burner in the kitchen. Why would you do so on such a hot night? I can't think of a good reason to do so, can you? Nobody comes home and thinks, isn't it hot I'll put on the AC, then goes into the kitchen to light the oven and bake a cake. I think we'd better go and have a look in the kitchen."

The went back into the kitchen. In among the old stove's ashes they found four metals buttons off a lady's shirt and the remains of two brass rims from fired shotgun rounds.

"Well, well," said Clark carefully removing the items with a pair of kitchen tongs and placing them into evidence bags. "She did do it. How can we prove it in court?"

Alice was puzzled, "the button's sir?"

"She probably got blood on herself and burnt her clothes after she cleaned herself up. We already knew she had taken a shower."

"Do we?"

"Yes, when I washed my hands in the en-suite on Tuesday night the towels were wet, but you remember how hot it was all day. If someone had taken a shower in the morning the towels would have been dry by the evening. Therefore, it stands to reason, someone had showered during the afternoon."

"Can we use any of this as evidence?"

"It's a crime scene, and Mrs McKay invited us in so I don't see why not. It's not like we've forced locks or anything. It's circumstantial anyway, it doesn't prove she did the murder, we need more than a few burnt buttons and a wet towel to take this further. Time for another chat with her I think. Let's get some officers go and pick her up while we go and speak to her sister."

"There is one more odd thing that's bugging me sir. Why would she move the body here to their home? Wouldn't it be easier to just dump it somewhere else? Do you think she wanted something from here to set up her little jilted lover scene?"

"Such as?"

"Well," speculated Alice, "maybe a change of clothes for him, or maybe just access to his guns because she wanted to disguise the wound."

"That's possible, but my guess is it gives her a reason to discover the body. If he was in a ditch somewhere she wouldn't be sure when the body was found. This way she had a chance to establish an alibi."

"But I didn't think she had an alibi," pointed out Alice.

"I know," said Clark, "and that's what's bugging me."

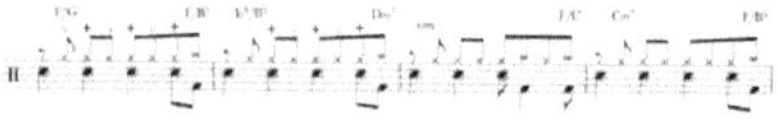

While Emma McKay always aimed at being stylishly presented, although arguably a little too heavily made-up, her sister Jeannie Jones resembled a refugee from Woodstock; her wardrobe and ethnic beaded neckless reminiscent of the late 1960's summer of love. It was unmistakable they were sisters; they shared similar features and many of the same facial expressions, but where Emma had worked hard to manicure her appearance to what societies norms considered to be her conventional best, Jeannie had embraced all her imperfections and simply gone from there.

Her house had done the same. When compared to her sisters the first and most obvious difference was its modest size. But it was on closer inspection the true character of the two homes displayed their important differences. Emma's house was rigorously traditional, Jeannie's had an eccentricity of spirit in keeping with her vibrant individualism. A statue of cupid stood in front of the house, on what no doubt once had been a lawn, but was now an attempt to grow some sort of a wildflower meadow in her front yard. The garden was dominated by an old tobacco shed now served as a garage, its outside painted in one large vivid mural. A mosaic pathway led up to the front door where a large wind chime acted as a doorbell.

Introductions were made, and refreshments were offered; herbal tea and a home baked biscuit, gluten and dairy free. The interior of the house was as eclectic as the outside. Tribal art rubbed shoulders unassumingly with Pre-Raphaelite reproductions. None of the furnishings matched in design or fabric and yet everything's total lack of coordination in no way jarred, being held together by the warm lighting and a sense of homeliness.

When they were seated inside, Clark looked at Alice and signalled he wanted her to start the questions. The answers came as fast as the questions in a brisk, rhythmic call and response; Clark listened to its tones and melodies focusing on only Jean's half of the conversation.

Yes, of course she knew Donald had been murdered. - ♪d#

No, she hadn't an alibi. - ♪d#

No, she wasn't with Frank Young. - ♪a

Yes, she knew who he was.

No, she wasn't having an affair with him. - ♪d#

No, neither was her sister - ♪c.

Yes, she had a relationship with Donald McKay years ago.

No, it wasn't an affair, she wasn't married at the time.

Don't be so bourgeois and judgemental. - ♪ d#

No, past tense. - ♪ d#

Yes, she was sure Emma knew all about it.

No, it was all over long ago.

Yes, she had seen his will. - ♪d

No, not before his death.

No, she couldn't prove that, how could she?

No, she discovered about May Richardson by reading the will. - ♪ d#

No, she didn't own a gun.

Yes, she could shoot one; you just pull the trigger, don't you?

No, she didn't own a car either, she had an old vespa instead. - ♪ d#

Yes, her husband owned one.

Yes, she could drive. - ♪ d

No, she didn't say she couldn't, just she didn't have her own car.

No, she hadn't seen her sister for about three weeks.

No, that wasn't unusual, they weren't close. - ♪ e

Yes, that was the last time she'd seen Donald as well.

And so, the conversation continued, Alice asking questions and Jeannie snapping back short replies to the ultimate benefit of neither party.

"Well," asked Alice once they were back in the car. "What did you make of her?"

"She's all over the place, fast answers, slow answers, angry answers, high pitched answers, a bit of everything. I can't get a read on her."

"My instincts tell me she's lying, and that could mean one of two things; either she was still having an affair, or she murdered him."

Clark pointed out they were, "Not mutually exclusive possibilities, but there is another possibility too."

"But," asked Alice, "you don't think she did it?"

"No, I don't, my money is still on Emma McKay," confirmed Clark, adding, "and I still think we'll find May Richardson is somehow part of the motive."

"But you think she was lying, don't you?"

"Perhaps," suggested Clark, "she's just a lot less bohemian than she makes out. My gut tells me she feels more than a little guilty about having slept with her brother-in-law."

Trouble, trouble
I've had it all my days
It seems like trouble
Going to follow me to my grave
Lovie Austin and Alberta Hunter

Luca had a slow and yet productive morning. His initial review of the motel carpark video footage had been next to useless. All he had been able to see was that Mrs McKay's car had driven past the motel on her way into Wangaratta at 9:11am and her husband's only four minutes behind her. His car never reappeared on the recording, but she could clearly be seen going home at 6:23pm. The recording also showed the delivery van Alice had talked about going past twice, five minutes either side of 2:30pm; this little piece of evidence confirming the sergeant's estimates while adding nothing new to the investigation.

Luca's own idea about the cameras in the high street shops had also failed to progress the investigation. While pedestrians were clearly visible walking past the jeweller's window, the camera angle was wrong to cover the cars on the road. He didn't have enough time to look through all the footage for any showing Emma McKay out shopping on Tuesday morning, but he took a copy of the video and would ask the sergeant if she wanted him to look through it all later.

After visiting the jewellery store, he walked down the street looking for other shops which had cameras. The high street was busy, customers crowding the pavements, returning for their retail therapy after weeks of on-line shopping. The town's commercial buzz was in contrast to its sometimes-sleepy rural atmosphere. He found another couple of cameras, but the only shop which did have a camera giving a clear view of the traffic had already deleted the recording, they said they only keep any footage for 48 hours so he should have come yesterday.

It was all starting to get very frustrating and a less determined officer may have been put off. Instead he had driven out to the roadworks where he had noticed a sign saying *40 Road Works* and a second claiming there was a *Traffic Management Camera* on trips out to Willow Cottage. Speaking to the site foreman however revealed there wasn't actually any camera there at all, the traffic workmen just put up a sign advertising one to slow the cars down. Just another case of false advertising.

His other idea, about tracing Mr McKay's movements using the Department of Health's Covid QR contact tracing system, had a different frustrating outcome. Apparently, while the contact tracing system could obviously go from a given venue to trace when people were there, he had been told although they could find out the information, they would not give it to him without a court order; it was against the states data privacy law. He had tried to circumvent his disappointment in being prevented from accessing the data by disclosing to them he was trying to track a murder victim who, being dead, clearly wasn't going to sue them for breach of privacy. Unfortunately, this had not changed their policy or advanced his case.

So, almost as a last resort, he had actually gone down to the café and seen their physical attendance register. Persistence is a virtue, and virtue brings a reward. For Luca, his reward came in the form of Donald McKay's name being clearly legible on the café's Covid sign in sheet. According to their Covid register he and his wife had sat down to have lunch together at 1:55pm. Luca showed the waitress a photograph of Donald McKay. She did not remember seeing him, but there it was, a record of him being there in old fashioned black and white. By this stage, Luca was feeling as if he was finally getting somewhere. Many, less diligent young detectives, would have left it there, but Luca was more meticulous than most. He decided to take his investigation further and checked the menu. Nachos were not listed. He enquired about this week's chalkboard specials; according to the waitress, nachos had not been served there for several weeks. Donald McKay may have been there at 1:55 but, as Luca deduced from this investigation, he must have eaten his lunchtime Nachos somewhere else.

The more difficult it seemed; the more determined Luca became. He'd find some trace of where he ate lunch, even if he had to go to every café in town. But where to start? He walked down the high street but none of those cafés recognised him from Luca's picture. He double checked using their paper Covid registers, but he hadn't manually signed their contact logs either. But he must have bought lunch somewhere, and Nachos aren't a good take away food, so, reasoned Luca, he must have sat down somewhere to eat them. He took out his phone and decided to resort to Google. It took him less than five minutes to bring up the menu for *The Railway Café*, a wholefood and organic eatery, only minutes down the road, with Mexican dishes as the house speciality.

Uniformed officers had brought Mrs Emma McKay into the station for questioning at 4:16pm. She was accompanied by her son-in-law who was acting as her lawyer. She was not under arrest, there being a big difference between believing someone is a murderer and having enough evidence to lay charges, and yet Clark's mind was already pivoting towards gathering proof rather than looking for alternative suspects.

On the way to question her, he stopped momentarily to keep his boss in the loop.

Teddy asked the obvious question, "How sure about her are you, Clark?"

"Not very to be honest, there is no real evidence, only she has lied about her movements all along, including this business about having lunch with her husband. Normally, not having lunch together isn't very suspicious, so why lie about it? Young Constable Bastoni found that little gem out, Donald had already eaten down the road and the Covid logs of them both having lunch together her have been falsified. I just can't see who else it could be at this stage."

"So, Luca's doing well, is he?"

"We've got him in hand Sir. Alice is going to make a policeman of him yet."

"Well, you be very careful with this one Clark. The press are on our case on this one, and Mrs McKay knows a lot of important people. Don't stuff this up."

The interview room at Wangaratta police station was painted an institutional grey; it smelled of disinfectant. The walls were bare, with two exceptions, a no smoking sign and a poster on the wall informing people of their rights along with the phone number of the nearest legal-aid office. There were no windows lighting being provided by a harsh fluorescent tube flickering occasionally. In the centre of the room stood an unadorned steel table with two chairs on each side. The only other items in the spartan chamber were a surveillance camera, to monitor proceedings fastened on the wall, and a microphone on the desk to record the interview.

Those unfortunate enough to find themselves there were left with no illusion about being within the clutches of an unsympathetic legal system.

After taking their positions on opposing sides of the table, Alice explained they intended to record the interview, and then asked everyone to state their name for the benefit of the recording. Once they had done so, Clark commenced the questioning by repeating the formal caution.

"For the record, I must inform you, you do not have to say or do anything but anything you say or do may be given in evidence. Do you understand that?"

Emma McKay confirmed she did by stating simply, "yes, I do," sounding as if she was restating her marriage vows.

Clark continued, "I must also inform you of the following rights; you may communicate with or attempt to communicate with a friend or a relative to inform that person of your whereabouts. You may communicate with or attempt to communicate with a legal practitioner. For the record I note your son-in-law Mr Colin Roberts is present, and he is a qualified legal practitioner. Do you wish to inform anyone or contact anyone else at this stage?"

"Not at the moment," she affirmed.

"And are you happy to continue with Mr Colin Roberts acting as your legal representative?"

"I am."

"Then we will proceed. As my Sergeant explained to you this interview is being taped. A copy or transcript of the interview can be made available to you or your legal representative on request."

"I understand all that, your Sergeant was very clear about it just now."

"Good. Can we please start by going over the events of last Tuesday? Let's begin with your leaving the house in the morning."

Mrs McKay sat back silently waiting, she looked over at her legal representative, and it was Colin Roberts who answered.

"Before we begin, I'd like to know, are you charging my client with anything?"

"At this stage we are just seeking a formal clarification of a few items in her previous statement in order to assist us in our enquiries."

"And how long do you intend to keep her here?"

"No longer than reasonably necessary to conduct this interview, unless she is subsequently charged with an indictable offence of course. However, given the serious nature of the offence, I don't think it unreasonable to ask for your client's continuing assistance, after all it is her husband's murder we are trying to solve."

Mrs McKay sat forward, placing her hand on her son-in-law's arm, she responded, "it's fine Colin, I've nothing to hide."

"And I would like to acknowledge, for the record, your client has been helpful so far in assisting us with her preliminary statement, as well as helping us earlier at her house."

"Of course, Inspector, and if I can help further, I will. So, to go back to your original question, I left the house at about nine thirty."

"What would you say if I was to tell you, you drove past the SunniSleep Motel on your way into town at 9:11am."

There was just enough there, thought Clark, to hint we know something she doesn't. Maybe even enough to unnerve her.

"Well, I may have got the time a bit wrong Inspector, I was going shopping, not trying to catch a train."

A good response, thought Clark, one has to admire her calmness, it's almost as if she has been questioned by police before.

"And Mr McKay."

"He'd finished his breakfast and was in his study getting a few papers. He had some business meeting he was getting ready for. I think he was seeing the bank. I really don't listen when he starts talking about the business."

Part of Clark's interview technique involved quickly changing the topic to keep his suspect off balance. Later he would revisit the original subject, like a jazz musician revisiting a song's melody line in his improvised composition. Each new variation gave Clark a chance to see if his suspect had changed their story, and all the time listening carefully with his trained musicians' ear to determine if they were lying.

"It says on the company's documents you are a shareholder and director."

"I'm sure that's true of a lot of wives, Inspector. A company legally needs two directors, and I have a few shares for tax reasons. Donald always ran the business."

Her answer was again coolly delivered, a response from a woman in control. Clark decided to flip back to the original line of questions to see if he could unnerve her.

"So back to Tuesday, you left the house after breakfast around nine, at which point your husband was alive and well."

"Correct."

Clark mentally noted the abruptness in her answer; one-word answers were generally a good sign of a suspect becoming defensive.

"Did you speak to him during the day at all, or perhaps send any text messages?"

"We're both a bit old for that sort of thing Inspector. I bet you don't text your wife during the day either, do you?"

And now, thought Clark, she's even asking me questions. I'm not getting anywhere fast here; I'd better pick up the tempo and change the key.

"As it happens, I'm not married. So, you didn't see him after breakfast?"

"I told you the other day, we had lunch together."

"Sorry of course you did, and that was what time?"

"Lunchtime. We often had lunch together when Donald was in town. Donald liked the Prelude Café at the Arts Centre."

Clark spotted another chance disrupt her imperturbable manner. He decided to see what she would do if he corrected her, and so he tried again.

"I think it's called Intermezzo actually, and you have a receipt from there?"

"I don't keep café receipts."

"And did the two of you have lunch with someone who could verify you were there?"

"Alone I'm afraid, but thinking about it we did sign in."

Which, thought Clark, is exactly where I'm about to go, but he decided it would be better to do so when he wanted to, and not follow her lead, so he asked something else first.

"And you're sure nobody can vouch for you?"

"Sorry Inspector."

"What would you say if I told you the Intermezzo Café's Covid sign in records show you and your husband were there at about five to two."

"That sounds right Inspector."

Good, thought Clark, feeling rather like a chess player who had tricked their opponent into putting one of their key pieces in jeopardy and could now spring a trap and capture it.

"And what would you say if I told you I have evidence proving your husband had his lunch at the Railway Café down the road?"

"Inspector," interrupted Colin Roberts, "can I have a word alone with my client?"

Damn, damn, damn, thought Clark. He had wanted her to respond and make a mistake, but now, like a boxer who had been saved by the bell, her answer would be carefully considered during this break and of little use to him.

Knowing he couldn't refuse; Clark suspended the interview as Mrs McKay went into a private discussion with her solicitor son-in-law.

The client-lawyer consultation only took around ten minutes, and soon, they were seated as before around the table discussing Mrs McKay's movements of the following Tuesday.

"My client," advised Colin Roberts, "would like to amend her previous statement."

"Inspector," added Mrs McKay. "On Tuesday my husband and I had coffee together, he had already eaten, and then he left to go to work."

"What time would that have been roughly?"

"I'm not sure, maybe I got the time wrong."

Clark measured the response, the interruption had spoilt his line of questioning, and as it was now, he had little option but to move on. He decided however, he should make one quick point before doing so.

"I just find it a little hard to believe, I'm afraid," he said.

Colin Reynolds interposed himself again, "what are you saying, it's just a little mix up over an exact time surely, nothing to prove my client has done anything else, Inspector."

"All I'm saying Mr Reynolds," explained Clark, "is normally when I arrange to meet someone, we generally specify when that will happen. I don't just show up randomly hoping whoever I'm meeting will just happen to be there at the same time. I'm therefore a little surprised your client is so vague about the time, but let's move on shall we. Mrs McKay can you tell me who paid please?"

"Pardon?"

Again, thought Clark, one word, defensive.

"Did you pay for these lunchtime coffees or did your husband?"

"I did Inspector."

"And was that usual?"

"Not really but I hadn't finished my lunch and he was in a bit of a hurry to get back to work after his coffee."

Clark could tell she was getting rattled but also knew it was not a topic where he could land a killer punch. He decided to change direction again. "Now, you said earlier you went to your daughter's house. Was it before or after lunch."

"Oh, in the morning sometime, before lunch."

"So, what time did you go home?"

"About six maybe, I can't remember looking at a clock, and I think we've established I'm not very good with times anyway. You probably know better than I do Inspector."

She's still enjoying this too much, thought Clark, it's as if she knows I haven't got enough to pin on her. Wondering what decisive piece of evidence he was missing; Clark continued.

"As it happens, I do, you drove up the road at 6:23pm. Were you in Wangaratta shopping all that time?"

"Well, most of the time, as I have already said, I went round to my daughters for a coffee as well."

"But before you had lunch with your husband?"

"Now, now, Inspector," she chastised him, "I think you mean coffee with my husband, which was at the Arts Centre around 2."

Now, realised Clark, she's even confident enough to be correcting me. This whole interview was beginning to seem like a bad idea.

"So, from shall we say quarter past two, after lunch anyway, you were shopping until about quarter past six, at which time you drove home."

"Yes."

"Although the shops shut at half five on a Tuesday."

"Not the supermarkets Inspector, they stay open until late all week."

"Only, you don't appear to have any receipts for the afternoon, and when I came on Tuesday evening there were no bags of new shopping waiting to be put away."

Since his previous interruption Colin Roberts had been sitting quietly making a few notes, but now he again interjected himself into the interrogation. "Inspector, I'm not sure where you are going with this latest fishing trip."

Neither do I, thought Clark.

"Firstly, Wangaratta isn't big a town. I'm not sure anyone could spend so many hours there just shopping, I know I couldn't, but let's assume for a moment your client can, then wouldn't it be reasonable to expect there to actually be some purchases, or did your client, for example, find her husband lying dead in the bedroom and then coolly just hang her new dresses up in the wardrobe as if nothing unusual had happened?"

"Haven't you heard of window-shopping, Inspector?"

"Not for a litre of milk and a loaf of bread I haven't. Did she put these mythical groceries away to tidy up the kitchen before we got there while her dead husband was upstairs?" Clark realised he was just clutching at straws, and perhaps being petty. Squabbling like this over nothing was not getting him anywhere. He needed to get the interview back on track; he had to return to some concrete facts he knew, so he could disprove her story. He turned to his suspect, "Mrs McKay can you furnish me with a list of the shops you visited, with approximate times if possible. Given you spent so long there, you should be on several Covid sign in sheets, and we can also ask if one of the many shop assistants you must have seen can remember you?"

"I'm afraid I can't Inspector, I can't really remember which shops I went into, and I must confess I'm not diligent about signing into shops either."

Clark knew he had scored another point but it still wasn't really getting him very far. "Okay, so you got home around half six, discovered your dead husband and then immediately phoned the station."

"I put the kettle on Inspector, went upstairs to change my shoes, where I found my husband, and then I phoned the police. I had probably been home five or ten minutes by then.”

Clark felt it was about time to go off on a tangent again, just to see if he could rattle her this time. Only he wasn’t sure in which direction he needed to go. Then, just like when at the piano he sometimes found himself playing through variations without having to think about each note, he heard himself almost subconsciously saying, “Do you know a Mr Francis Young, you may know him as Frank.”

“I know him Inspector.”

He could hear a shift in her voice, perhaps only a semitone, but it was there. He had scored his hit and unsettled her. The only trouble was, he really was fishing this time, and so he had no idea what it meant or where to go with this line of questions. A long time ago Teddy Edwards had told him the best questions in an interrogation were generally those you already know the answer to, only here, Clark was asking his questions blind, improvising. Nothing for it though, I’ve started, he thought, I’d better just play out the melody and see if I can turn it into a song.

“Your sister introduced you I understand.”

“Sort of, I met him once or twice at Jeannie’s house.”

“You see your sister often then?”

It was a nothing question, and Clark regretted it almost at once as she answered, “is that unusual Inspector?”

“Well, we have heard the two of you don’t get on.”

“I don’t know where you heard that, but it isn’t true.”

No, thought Clark, wrong question again, he wasn’t going to trick her into saying anything about Jeannie being Donald’s mistress by being this clumsy. He tried again.

“Okay, back to Mr Young. Did you see Mr Young at any time on Tuesday?”

"No."

And there it was again, a fractional hesitation, perhaps only discernible to a musician's ear; a false note played out of time. Clark felt his opponent was now tottering; a boxer near the ropes, if only he could land one good punch it would be all over. Would she oblige and supply him with an opening? He waited to see if she would elaborate. Sometimes as a technique it worked, but not with the really accomplished liar; the old lag who would just wait him out.

"Do you know what my girlfriend and I do when we want a quiet afternoon out together?" he asked her rhetorically. "We go out of town to a café somewhere, say Milawa, or Beechworth, somewhere where it's less likely anyone will recognise us, so it is bit more private. Do you and Mr Young have your own quiet spot?"

"Inspector?"

"Is that a 'no comment'? Because, you see, I think 'no comment' really means 'yes'. I know it makes you look bad. I know it gives you a motive. But I want you to consider this, it could also give you an alibi. So, I'll ask you again, did you see Mr Young at any time on Tuesday?"

"Alright, yes, we met up in the afternoon."

No! thought Clark, she gave up far too easily. It was almost as if she, who had laid a trap for him, not the other way. He felt as if he had asked her exactly the question she wanted him to, but now he had been tricked he had no choice but to continue.

"What time exactly."

By this stage in a normal interview Clark was used to being on top, but not with Emma McKay. He was floundering and knew it.

There was a mischievous twinkle in Emma McKay's voice as she answered, "Exactly Inspector?"

Clark heard it, and correctly thought, she's having fun now. She thinks she has won.

"As close as you can."

"After I'd had lunch with Donald."

There was a knock at the door and Luca Bastoni entered with a sheet of paper.

Good, thought Clark, relieved this time to hear the bell himself, convinced he was not getting anywhere. Maybe the interruption was his lifeline back into this little battle of wits. Mechanically he heard himself say, "For the benefit of the record Constable Luca Bastoni has just entered the room with a copy of a warrant issued today authorising the search of both Mr and Mrs McKays' cars. I also intend to search the residence again at the same time. Mrs McKay do you wish to attend or appoint a representative to attend on your behalf at the time of the search?"

Colin Roberts picked up the warrant. "Can I have another moment with my client?"

"Of course," said Clark looking at his watch, "interview suspended…sixteen forty-seven."

Clark and Alice left for a second time, again allowing their suspect and her lawyer to confer alone while they went outside with Luca Bastoni. Through the thick interview room door they could hear the muffled voice of their suspect and her concerned solicitor.

"Well?" enquired Alice.

"We aren't getting anywhere are we?" admitted Clark. "Let's get this search done and find a reason to suspend this whole thing. She's too old a hand at this sort of thing to crack without something concrete."

Mrs McKay's conversation with her solicitor was short and it was only a minute or two before Colin Roberts knocked on the door and invited them back into the room.

Alice performed the official announcements; "Interview with Mrs Emma McKay recommenced sixteen fifty-one, also present are Mr Colin Roberts acting as Mrs McKay's legal representative and conducting the interview are myself Senior Sergeant Alice Dees and Inspector Clark Reynolds. I must ask you Mrs McKay, formally and for the record, you have been served a warrant to search your car in connection with the death of your late husband Mr Donald McKay. We also intend to re-examine the crime scene, namely your house Willow Cottage, at the same time. Do you wish to be present or appoint a representative to be present during the search?"

"Yes, I want to be there, and I'd like Colin to be there too."

It was gone ten o'clock when Sergeant Mike Owen and his forensics officers had finished searching, vacuuming and generally sampling fibres from the boot and upholstery fabrics of Mrs McKay's and the late Mr McKay's cars. Neither had obvious signs of blood stains so now they would have to start the laborious process of comparing dozens of samples to those found in Mr McKay's hair to see if he had ever been in the boot. Matching any samples from the upholstery could of course be easily explained, but the boot was another matter.

"Now," said Clark, "Mrs McKay, can we please go inside?"

"How long is this going to take?"

"Well, we've already recovered some evidence from inside the house so it shouldn't take long. Do you mind unlocking the gun case for us?" asked Clark.

"I don't mind Inspector, but I can't, my husband was the only person who had a key," she explained, "and I'm afraid I don't know where he kept it."

"I'm not surprised to hear you say that," said Clark. He signalled to Mike Owen. "Sergeant!"

Sergeant Owen stepped forward with a drill and accompanied by the screeching noise of scraping metal; he proceeded to push out the lock.

Although the inside of the cabinet was large enough for several weapons it only contained two hunting rifles and assorted boxes of ammunition. One of the opened boxes was half full of shotgun cartridges.

Clark looked satisfied.

"Sergeant can you please dust; the door, guns, ammunition boxes and anything else for prints, and take samples of the shotgun cartridges for comparison with the shells I gave you earlier."

"What shells are those?" asked Colin Roberts.

"We recovered the remains of two cartridges from the fire in the kitchen during our previous search we believe may have been used to shoot Mr McKay."

"And when did you search for those, before or after getting a warrant."

"After being invited into the house by your client to investigate her husband's murder. Not only were we given permission by your client to search the house originally, but the house is, I shouldn't have to remind you, a crime scene. That's two good reasons why we don't need a warrant. If you recall, the warrant was to search the cars, to see if they are connected to the crime, particularly the transportation of Mr McKay's body."

"I think you are walking a fine line there, Inspector."

"Not really and I'm just doing my job. Criminal law is a bit different from divorces and conveyancing, isn't it? Don't you think you should be advising your client to get a specialist to represent her?"

"Perhaps I would if she wasn't innocent, then she'd need someone else, but as it is, why bother?

"Are you satisfied with your observations of the search and ready to recommence the interview?"

"It's been a very long day Inspector; can't we adjourn this ridiculous charade until tomorrow morning?"

Good, thought Clark to himself, I was kind of hoping you'd say that; it'll give us a bit of time to process the evidence.

"If you prefer," he said, trying to sound as if he was generously allowing a concession, before going on to say, "and to show my goodwill, I'm still not arresting your client. I'm happy to let her stay here tonight, and I'll arrange for an officer to collect her and bring her in first thing tomorrow morning. Of course, I'll also insist on having an officer stay outside in the meantime. I trust you have no objection."

On his way-out Clark had a quick word with Mike Owen about the forensic evidence.

"I'm going to question her again tomorrow and I really need something; will it give your team long enough to look at everything?"

"I'll do it first thing, but it will take a while, it could take a couple of days."

"Sooner will be better."

"I appreciate that Inspector. I'll do it as fast as I can, but I have to do it right."

"I know you will Mike, before you go, did you ever track down the size 10 boot?"

"Not specifically, it's just a pretty standard tread from a work boot; the sort tradies wear; you know steel toe-caps, elastic sides, nothing special."

"Could you match them to a particular pair?"

"Sometimes," admitted Mike, "but not often."

"I thought," enquired Clark, "you could from the particular wear pattern; things like a stone in the tread."

"I suppose in theory you can," explained the forensics sergeant, "but in practice work boots like these tend to get knocked about a lot, so you'd need to get bloody lucky."

"But if I got you a boot to compare it to?" asked Clark.

"I'd take a good look naturally, but until then it's all a bit academic anyway, isn't it?"

By the time Clark arrived home it was well past midnight. Despite the late hour Ella was pleased to see him.

"You're a good dog, aren't you? Would you like to live here with me all the time?"

Clark thought it had been a rhetorical question, but Ella showed she had understood by jumping up at him to show her approval.

"You shouldn't jump up at people Ella," he told her. "Now you be a good girl and I'll see what I can do. I suppose you need a walk before bed. Let's just take a short one then. It's been a long day, and I'm tired even if you aren't."

Clark woke earlier than he would have liked on account of having a puppy jump on him.

"Ella, get down. Now miss, you are not allowed in here, ever."

He took her into the kitchen and let her out into the back yard.

Still, he thought, I suppose it's better to be woken up by the dog than to wake up and discover she's gone to the toilet in the lounge overnight.

After a quick bowl of cereal for Clark, and a bowl of biscuits for Ella, Clark dressed to take Ella for a walk before breakfast.

On the way he phoned June.

"Hi, I've got a favour to ask."

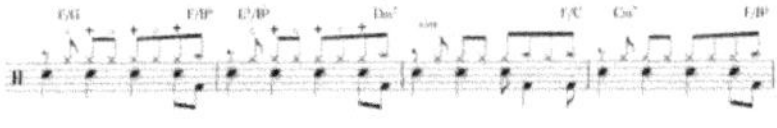

It was only a little before nine when Clark turned up at June's house with Ella. June was already in the garden, pottering among her assorted flower beds.

"Thanks for having her, I would have left her at home but she doesn't know it's her home yet, and she was there most of the day alone yesterday."

"What would you have done," asked June reasonably, "if I had said I was very busy?"

"I'd say you were talking rubbish," explained Clark, "you never work weekends."

"There's more to life than work," explained June.

"I know. I'll owe you one," Clark promised.

"So, you're keeping her then?"

"I think so. Tommo in the dog unit says he'll do me a good deal."

"It's a big commitment," observed June.

"What do you mean, I'm Mr Commitment and anyway," said Clark, "you like German Shepherds anyway. You told me."

"When?"

"The other day, you said you wanted to get one."

"I really don't remember ever saying that."

"I suppose it depends on you really, I guess. She's a nice dog though, toilet trained already; woke me at about five this morning to be let out."

"You're really not selling this idea to me. Leave her with me today and I'll add it to the list of things you owe me for," she said. "We'll talk about it later. Just make sure you come straight round after work." She paused, bending over to pick up a stick for Ella, before continuing, "and you're right I'm not on call unless there is another suspicious death I have to attend, and that would be your fault anyway."

"You're a life saver, sometimes I don't know what I'd do without you."

"Remember that thought. Do you want to come in and have a coffee before you go?"

"I shouldn't really, I'm supposed to be interviewing a suspect, but you know what. Let her wait and stew for a bit. I'm not even sure I know what I'm supposed to be asking her anyway, and I'd love a coffee."

As he was following her inside his phone rang.

"I've just got to get this first and then I'll be straight in."

Mike Owen was well known for his hard work but even so Clark was not expecting his call so early in the morning.

"Clark?"

"Morning Mike, you've got good news I take it."

"Nothing 100% definitive but I'm just looking at the car samples."

"And?"

"They are not the same car fibres."

Clark knew Mike had a reputation for meticulous detail, the call, before he had completed his examination, was therefore a little out of character.

"Are you sure?"

"Like I said," explained Mike, "nothing 100% yet, I've only just started, but your victim had short straight synthetic fibres on him, and these are twisted; both these cars have wool carpets."

"Couldn't it be some sort of blend?" suggested Clark.

"I doubt it. I'll have one of the lads go through all the other samples, but I'm confident we'll find he wasn't in the boot of either of those cars, or if he was, he was all wrapped up in a sheet and there's no forensics."

"What about the house, has anyone looked at the fingerprints on the gun case or ammunition box yet."

"Getting prints off a cardboard box takes time, it's not just like dusting a doorhandle. When we've got something, I'll call."

"Thanks Mike, not what I wanted to hear, but thanks."

Inside June poured Clark a coffee and was just asking what time he was hoping to be able to come round later when Clark suddenly interrupted her.

"June, have you got the images from the neck wound?"

"Yes, my draft report is still over on the desk."

Clark walked over and flicked through the pictures looking for the one labelled 'neck wound.'

"This washed sand," he asked, "was it only on his neck?"

June considered this for a moment. "Yes, I see what you mean. If he was dragged across a sandy building site he'd be covered in sand and scratches, but he isn't. Actually, there are no signs of a fight. It's like he was stabbed and fell straight down, or maybe fell over and was stabbed before he had a chance to get up."

"And?"

"And that means the sand was more than likely on the murder weapon that killed him. If I was you, I'd be looking for a tool on a building site, something like a brickies trowel maybe; something blunt anyway."

"Was there anything else on the body to tell us more?"

"Well, my technician, Pratibha, identified some lead carbonate hydroxide under his nails."

"What's that?" Clark asked.

June wracked her brain, "I think it's used in white paint."

"Which just suggests a building site again," dismissed Clark disappointedly.

"I don't think so, nobody has used lead in paints for decades."

"Well," suggested Clark, "he did live in an old house, maybe he had an old tin lying around."

"That's what I thought too, only Pratibha said it wasn't old dry paint."

"So, who still uses lead paint?" asked Clark.

"I don't know, maybe lead carbonate is used for something else these days."

June took out her phone and after typing a few words started to read from the screen. "Lead carbonate hydroxide was formerly used as an ingredient for lead paint, pottery and as a 16th century cosmetic called Venetian ceruse. White lead compounds known as lead soap were also used as an additive for lubricants in machine shops. Oh, this is interesting, the Royal Navy used it to protect their timber ships from shipworm. I think that's a sort of mollusc. Anyway, it says here because of its tendency to cause lead poisoning, its use in paint has now been banned in most countries. There is a reference here to an international paint convention in 1921."

"Like I said." repeated Clark, "it's an old house, easily older than 1921, so there could just be an old tin in the shed. I'll make a note to check next time I'm out there."

Clark kissed June goodbye and gave Ella a pat. As he left, he called over his shoulder, "Be a good girl and I'll see you later."

June was left unsure which of the two of them he was addressing.

Knock, knock.

What was that, thought Luca; he stepped out of the shower.

Knock,

Oh, it's the door. Who could be knocking this early?

Knock, knock

"Yes, yes, I'm coming!"

He wrapped the damp towel around his middle, and went to answer it leaving wet footprints while trying hard not to slip on the polished boards. Only half opening the door, so he could hide himself from view, he peered through the crack to reveal Alice.

"What's up?"

"And good morning to you too Constable. What a wonderful day to be up bright and early and ready to go."

"It's my day off."

"In which case you should be free from commitments and up for a bit of an expedition"

Luca gave an exasperated sigh, "five minutes."

"It's okay," said Alice stepping through the doorway, "I'll just wait in here."

Luca shared his flat with two other twenty something men, one of whom, like Luca, worked in the police service. It was a short term furnished rental and came with the sort of pine furniture which requires an Allen key and Scandinavian assembly instructions; its battered nature suggested it had not been redecorated since the 1970's. On the wall hung a tired embroidered picture of orange poppies, either a brilliant piece of retro decorating or something from a Bermuda Triangle time warp of bad taste.

As Luca turned towards his bedroom to get dressed, he clearly heard Alice say, "nice," and hoped she was talking about the décor.

True to his word Luca was ready in minutes, partly through the expedient practice of not shaving on his day off. To Alice's relief, given the dated interior design of the flat, he was not wearing flared trousers.

"So, Sarge, where are we going?"

"Well, we've still got to tidy up a few loose ends, let's get over and see Pete King before the boss gets in."

"Isn't it too early?"

"He's a farmer," explained Alice, "he doesn't keep office hours. Let's go."

Alice was right, on their arrival Pete King was already up and about in the yard, and standing next to a quad bike. It was an old machine without a roll over cage and he was busy strapping tools onto the tray at its rear.

She introduced herself, "Good morning Mr King we're police officers; we'd like to ask you a few questions, if you've got a minute."

Pete King briefly looked up at Alice before continuing with his work.

Unfazed, Alice continued, "can you confirm where you were early Tuesday afternoon?"

"Don't know." His answer contained as few syllables as he could muster. It Pete King had been the sort of man to know what laconic meant, then it would have been a suitable description, as it was however, he was rude.

Alice persisted, "between one and say four in the afternoon."

"Look, I haven't time for this now."

"Mr King," interrupted Luca, "we can do this informally here now, or if you like you can come with us down the station and do it there. It's up to you."

Alice nodded to Luca, encouraging him to continue.

"So, like my Sergeant asked you, where were you between one and four o'clock on Tuesday?"

"I was down the river paddock all day doing a bit of fencing."

"And from there do you have a view of Willow Cottage?"

"I suppose I did."

"In which case," asked Luca, "did you see anyone coming or going about midday or early afternoon?"

"There was a white van I think, lunchtime, just came and went."

"Anyone else?"

"Not that I recall. Well…" He stopped in midsentence.

"So, you did see someone?" encouraged Luca.

"Well, there was a little car, I think."

"Can you remember anything about it."

"I think it was a little red and white job, like a Fiat. You know, those little hatch back things they drive in town."

"And that was definitely Tuesday."

"I'm not saying definite, no, come to think it could have been Monday."

"Did many people used to come and go," asked Luca listing the names, "Jeannie Jones, Frank Young, Dedra Fernton, Stevie Dunn?"

"Don't know them," admitted Pete King before correcting himself by saying, "well I know Jeannie of course, but it wasn't her car; she rides an old vespa; makes a noise like a sewing machine; frightens the sheep."

On their way back to the station Luca asked, "Why was he so rude to you?"

"That's nothing," explained Alice. "I'm used to much worse than him."

"Well, you shouldn't have to put up with it."

"Thank you," she said sincerely, "but the world's full of racists and sexists. He is probably both, but you can't change the world. You know the funny thing, and maybe I shouldn't say this now…"

"Go on," Luca encouraged.

"When I first met you, I thought you were a bit of a bigot too."

"Well," said Luca, "you were probably right," and he apologised, "sorry." Before Alice could reply he added, "where too now?" in order to change the topic.

"I can either drop you at your home Constable, and you can enjoy your day off watching football on the TV, or whatever thrilling day you had planned, or if you prefer, we can go to the station and catch a murderer."

Arriving at the station late Clark was met by Alice.

"Morning Sir, we've got Mrs McKay in interview room 2 waiting."

"Thank you Alice, but can you get her a coffee and make her wait for a bit. We will need to talk to her again, but she isn't going to confess anytime soon, so we will need to do this from a different angle."

Alice seemed a little confused. "Are you sure sir? Last night we both thought she was guilty."

"Well, I still do, but we just don't have enough to charge her with yet. I think we will need some good forensics first. Let's wait until Mike gets back to us before speaking to her. We may even have to let her go today and put the interview off. Is Luca in?"

"He's on the phone."

Clark went into the general office and stood over Luca as he was talking, mouthing he wanted a word in his office.

Luca put up his hand signalling he wanted the inspector to stay.

"Look my Inspector is here now, can you tell him what you just told me…I'll hand you over."

Luca tried to pass Clark his phone, but Clark just pressed the speaker button so they could both still hear.

"Morning," called Clark, "I am Inspector Clark Reynolds of the Victorian North East Division."

The voice on the other end was of a young woman, knowledgeable, authoritative.

"Inspector, I understand you are looking for a couple of stolen paintings. As I was just informing the Constable, I think I've located them. A Melbourne dealer has been trying to sell two pictures, fitting the details, privately. The dealer is someone we have come across before, not one to double check a provenance."

"Do you know who he bought the pictures from?"

"He doesn't own them, he is selling them on behalf of someone else, it's a woman from up your way actually, a Mrs Sarah Roberts of 42…"

Clark interrupted her before she could complete the address, "yes, I know Mrs Roberts, and her connection to this matter."

"You may know her, but this may be new to you. Would you be interested to learn, and I haven't had the pictures formally examined by our people yet you understand, but they came to our attention not as stolen pictures but as possible fakes. I have spoken to an expert from Sydney University, professor Dr David Boothby, who assures me at least one of the pictures is an obvious forgery, and the other he is currently unsure about as well. He said, a collector he works on behalf of was offered the pictures and he advised her not to proceed with the purchase as they were very dubious. His advice was, at this stage, we should be treating them both as fake."

"Are there many fake Heidelberg school pictures doing the rounds?"

"Not just doing the rounds Inspector, there's some in major collections. Nobody these days would dare to try and pass a Raphael or Titian as genuine, but Tom Roberts is considered fair game, I'm afraid."

"But you are sure these two are the same two stolen on Tuesday."

"Well, I've got a colleague at the dealer this morning as it happens to check. He could send you a photo of the pictures on his phone if you like and you can have a look yourself, or I'll e-mail his inspection report through later, but I'm pretty sure they are at this point."

"I wouldn't know what I was looking at, but if you could send me your experts report it could be useful, thank you. Do you have all the insurance photos to compare them to?"

"All in the original report your Constable sent me."

"Let me know, as soon as you can, if they are the same pictures. They could just be copies of the two originally insured. We could still have a couple of genuine originals floating around somewhere we need to locate. I suspect though we are only dealing with a couple of fakes here, I don't see Sarah Roberts forging art; I've seen a couple of her pictures and, well, they aren't her style."

"When the pictures are in custody, we'll do some tests to see how old they are, I've got an expert coming in later today. I should be able to let you know more this afternoon."

"While I've got you, can I ask you about white paint?"

"Are you asking in general, or are we still talking about the Heidelberg school?"

"Well," said Clark, "I was thinking generally, but let's start with what sort of paint those artists use."

"I don't know, flake white I expect. Maybe zinc white, that was around then as well, I don't think any artist used Titanium white until the 1920's. There are a few other whites too, but they weren't very common then. Do you want me to ask our expert?"

"It may be helpful. When you say *flake,* do you mean lead?"

"That's right," said the young expert, excited by the rare chance to talk professionally about her specialty, "you make it by corroding lead plates in pots suspended above vinegar and burying it all in compost. After a few months the lead ends up as papery white crystals which you mix with oil to make paint. It's actually a fascinating process."

"Can you still buy lead white?"

"In Australia? Yes you can. Some manufactures use modern methods, but I know of one company in the UK that still produce it in small batches the old-fashioned way and sells it here. It's very expensive compared to modern pigments but a few artists are prepared to pay the extra and use it, as well as museums for restorations, of course."

"If I wanted to buy some here in Wangaratta, could I?"

"I don't know what sort of art supply shops you have locally but the internets a wonderful thing Inspector, I'm sure you could get it mail order."

After the conversation had finished, and Clark had said "well done" to Luca, he asked Alice to go and bring Frank Young in for another round of questioning.

"What else do we have to do, sir?" asked Alice.

"When you've got Frank, then you can get onto Mike Owen again, I just need to know whose fingerprints if any are inside the gun case."

"What do you want me to do about Mrs McKay?"

"Let her stew for the morning. We'll have to let her go in an hour or so but I'll inconvenience her for as long as I can. It's the least I can do for her husband."

You're mean to me
Why must you be mean to me?
Gee, honey, it seems to me
You love to see me cryin'

Fred Ahlert and Roy Turk

Clark sat at the piano in the living room tinkering a tune with one hand while sipping his coffee with the other. To his relief Ella rested by his feet; she was not one of those dogs who annoyingly tries to join in whenever they hear music. The score for *The Second Time Around* sat open in front of him, and he started to play. He played because the notes were there in front of him, and because the gaps between the notes were empty and needed filling. Most of all he played as a meditation. And that's when it happened; the musical ideas flashed through his head as he started improvising, the notes flowed rapidly from his fingers forming multiple thoughts and then fading in quick succession. First a part of a scale, and then a musical phrase, up and down like the waves in the ocean, slowly forming a pattern never seen before, and which will never be exactly the same again. A murder had a rhythm and a melody too, and Clark rode those threads like the tempo of the tune. The song gave his brain the freedom to trample the mundane world of interviews and witness statements; allowed him to break free of the case's gravity, and as he did, all the places he'd been in the past few days flashed past one by one; Willow Cottage, the bedroom, its en-suite, the hallway, the kitchen, Sarah's house and her garden studio, only they were no longer locations and clues to him, they were quavers and crotchets on a score, and as he sat at the

180

piano, he instinctively played their song arranging the pieces into a pattern as decipherable as the one on the page in front of him.

June recognised the expression on his face, she had seen it many times before, when he was accompanying her sing.

"You know," she stated. It was not a question but a recognition of his sudden clarity.

He exchanged a look with her, and simply said, "I almost missed it. Sometimes," he admitted, "I miss what's right in front of me."

"I've noticed that," she observed.

"Well, I know what happened; I'd better go and arrest her then."

Before leaving he phoned his constable.

"Luca, you're one of these young social media types." He couldn't help the slight sound of judgement creeping into his voice, disapproval.

"Well, I'm not exactly a social influencer, but I am younger than you are sir if that's any help."

"Well Luca, I've a job for you," continued Clark. "In the evidence box you'll find a bag with some burnt buttons; they look like they are made of brass, you can't miss them. I want you to go through all Sarah Robert's Facebook posts and find me a picture of her wearing a shirt, dress, something with those buttons on. Come on," he encouraged Luca, momentarily sounding uncharacteristically rather like a football coach giving his team a half-time talk, "we're almost there with this one."

By the time they had arranged a warrant it was already early afternoon before they arrived at Sarah Roberts' house. Sarah, her mother and husband were all home.

The warrant was not unexpected but met with the cursory protests of mock outrage anyway.

"And what exactly are you looking for Inspector?"

"Well, let's start with your car please Mrs Roberts, and we'll just see what we can find."

"I'd love to help," claimed Sarah, "but unfortunately it was stolen yesterday."

"Just before we looked in your mother's car boot I suppose?" asked Clark sarcastically, sounding rather like his friend Tom did when telling off an errant student failing to hand in their homework.

"Inspector?"

"Have you reported it?"

"Yes, I've got a reference number somewhere."

"I'll look at it later," said Clark. "let's just start with your studio instead, shall we?"

Sarah led the procession down the garden path to her modest studios, avoiding the recently poured concrete of her new patio. It was a timber prefabricated kit building, but had been fitted with extra windows in the ceiling to make it light and airy. There was a distinct smell of linseed oil and disinfectant, together with something else Clark couldn't readily identify."

"You've been cleaning," Clark observed.

"Of course, Inspector. You need to keep a clean studio."

The forensics officer accompanying them during the search donned a pair of orange glasses and preceded to spray luminol solution over the floor and walls, all the while shining a uv torch backwards and forwards.

"Here we go," he announced, "blood."

Clark borrowed his special glasses so he could see too. Satisfied, by the evidence they revealed, he began to recite his legal liturgy, "Sarah Roberts I am arresting in connection to the murder of Mr Donald McKay you do not have to say anything but …"

Alice's interview with Frank Young had not gone in the way Emma McKay had hoped for. Frank's story had chopped and changed as he had become increasingly willing to cooperate as the interview progressed.

Alice's interview technique was quite distinct from the approach Clark took. She liked to ease a suspect into the conversation, a softly, softly approach more akin to a priest in a confessional than a police interrogation; she offered him a coffee. Her first question was to simply ask him to tell her about his relationship with Emma McKay.

"So, how do you know Emma?"

Over the years Frank had been interviewed by the police on numerous occasions but had never been invited into the station for one of Alice's informal chats before. His response remained guarded, he hardly knew Emma McKay, they had met a few times but not on Tuesday when, he had spent the day gardening. It was the same story he had told Clark, but one that contradicted Emma's own account.

Alice continued, again she referred to Mrs McKay by her given name, keeping the chat as relaxed as possible, "really, because I spoke to Emma and she said you two had a thing."

There was no judgement in her voice keeping the interview as close to two old friends chatting about their latest boyfriends as she could.

"Yeah, we have seen a bit of each other lately I guess."

"What's the Golden Leaf Hotel up in Beechworth like?"

There it was, just enough information to let him know what Emma had told her without accusing him of anything wrong, and certainly nothing asking him what sort of man cheats on four wives, just two old friends catching up.

"Nice, we've been there a few times."

It was an unusual interview technique but soon Alice had Frank admitting both a long-standing affair, and that he was with her for most of the afternoon, having met up shortly after lunch. At this point Frank seemed to remember he was speaking to a police officer and asked to call his lawyer.

Alice, had no option but to suspend the interview, which she did gracefully as if to say, "well you can't blame a girl for trying."

In her time as a successful divorce solicitor Margot Brice-Jones had only seen the inside of Wangaratta Police Station's interview rooms on a handful of occasions and her attendance today was at first sight an odd choice for Frank to make. Her Porsche, classic Chanel suit and slimline snakeskin briefcase all suggested her inflated billing rate. When a client paid her fee they usually won.

By the time they were ready to recommence Alice had spoken to Clark.

"He's lawyering up Sir, do you want to sit in?"

"I'm sure it's nothing you can't handle, just let him know it's Emma we're after. You'll be fine."

Alice restarted the interview.

"So Frank, is there something you want to tell me?"

In response Margot Brice-Jones informed her that "My client was with me on Tuesday afternoon. He attended a meeting with a third party to discuss that person's business,"

"At this stage we are not investigating your client, however we are very interested in his connection to Mrs Emma McKay. Was she at this meeting?"

"I'm afraid that is privileged information so I am not in a position to say who the third party was without speaking to them first."

"Can you at least tell me the time of this meeting?"

Margot Brice-Jones consulted with her client before answering, "Four o'clock."

"In that case," exclaimed Alice, "I'm not actually interested anyway. Mr McKay was long dead by then."

"But why," asked Frank, "would Emma take me to a divorce lawyer if she knew her husband was dead?"

"To make it look as if she didn't already know he was dead."

"That doesn't make sense, she asked me not to say anything."

"Your right," agreed Alice, "it wouldn't make sense if she actually thought that you wouldn't say anything, but she obviously knew that you would. So, let's go back to your liaison earlier in the day at the hotel in Beechworth."

"Can I have a minute with my lawyer?"

"I imagine she's charging by the hour, so I suppose so. Do you want me to suspend the interview?"

Soon Alice was going through the events again pointing out how often Frank had changed his story, after which he then told her how Emma McKay had coached him how and when to swap stories. It was all her idea he said, "only say we were together when they push you. If you make it seem you are reluctant, they'll find it more believable."

Most of all he stated he had not seen Emma McKay earlier in the day, he had not spent the afternoon in a hotel with her, and he had received a phone call from her at half past three asking him to meet her at the solicitors.

"And," asked Alice, "are you willing to sign a formal statement to that effect?"

"If you like."

Alice turned to his solicitor, "I've got a question for you if you don't mind."

"And how can I help you."

"This meeting you had with your client and an unconfirmed third party, who your client tells me was Emma McKay?"

"What do you want to know?"

"I was wondering when it was booked?"

"I'm not sure, I think it was a spur of the moment thing. I'd have to ask my assistant."

"If you would."

And while Margot Brice-Jones was confirming that the meeting had in fact only been arranged at short notice on Tuesday, Alice took down her client's final statement. It was an account that for all his small-time criminal record and felonious exaggerations showed that Frank had no intention of becoming an accessory to murder; not by providing a false alibi for Emma McKay at any rate. His own freedom it appeared was valued much more than his relationship with Emma McKay. Perhaps, on reflection, given he had two wives waiting for his safe return to the commune, both ready to help console his double-crossing conscience, it should not have really surprised her.

Standing either side of Alice's whiteboard, Clark Reynolds and Luca Bastoni slowly started going through the evidence. Clark knew he had made a mistake questioning Emma McKay before collating enough data and was keen not to repeat his error when interviewing her daughter, Sarah. She had already surprised them once by asking her husband not to represent her and was currently in the cells awaiting the arrival of the legal aid lawyer. Before he came, they had one last chance to go through the case.

They had acquired various pieces of evidence against her.

Firstly, and perhaps most significantly, her studio had been the apparent scene of the murder. There were signs of blood on both the floor and walls. This would need DNA checking later, just to confirm whose blood it was, of course, but Clark had no doubt it belonged to Donald McKay.

Added to that she used the same high quality lead white artists oil paint matching the paint found under his fingernails. As this was not readily available locally, and not even widely used by artists, its presence was strongly indicative he had been there on the day of his murder.

Then there was the fact, that a small set of probably woman's fingerprints had been found inside the gun case. Mike Owen's team were still running a full comparison, a process which could take several days, but a quick look at the overall pattern, a mixed one of whorls and arches, was similar to Sarah's and quite distinct from her mother's. Not conclusive without the full analysis, Clark had to admit, but at this point Clark wasn't going to let that stop him. She had said, the first time Clark ever spoke to her, she couldn't identify the gun because she never went shooting, yet her fresh prints appeared inside the locked gun case. Again, this alone was not decisive, there was any number of possible explanations how she, as a member of the family, could have come into contact with the gun case, but it was certainly another piece in the jigsaw.

Luca had also found out the burnt remains of the buttons found in the oven matched those from one of her blouses he had seen her wearing in numerous Facebook posts. Why would she have burnt the blouse unless it somehow incriminated her? It was illogical. If she merely wanted to get rid of it there were numerous easier ways. No, Clark was sure, the fact she destroyed it on the day, and at house, where the body was found was tantamount to an admission of her guilt.

Then there was the builders' sand in the wound; she was building a patio and barbeque in her garden. The lack of the actual weapon troubled him here he had to acknowledge, finding it would have tied it up nicely. He suspected it was under all the new concrete in the backyard somewhere, they could dig it up later. He was also a little puzzled by why she would be standing in the sun on a thirty plus day doing building work at all. Hopefully it would fall into place too.

Finally, a case of wine had been recovered from her house, labelled for Donald McKay, and which, according to the consignment sticker, was the same wine delivered on the day of the murder.

There was only one major piece of the puzzle missing: Sarah's car. So far although the description of the car had been circulated, they had been unable to locate it. Clark was sure however, that when they eventually tracked it down the lab would be able to confirm the car carpet fibres found in Donald's hair would be from its boot.

Going through the case with Luca strengthened the instinctive deductions he had made while playing the piano. He knew he had more than enough to question Sarah with.

Her confession had come easily, she expressed no guilt during it, just a sensation of relief, as if a burden had been lifted from her shoulders. Clark hardly had time to outline all of the evidence against her before she began talking. It sometimes happened that way, people who have been bottling so much inside them for days needing to spurt it all out, to tell their dark secret.

"It was that stupid tart's fault," Sarah began.

"You mean May Richardson?" asked Clark.

"Yes," she continued, "I saw the will of course. Mother showed it to Colin; she wanted a legal opinion about it you see. What did he mean she was his daughter; I was his daughter! What do I get? 25% of a business going bankrupt, is that all I'm worth? And then she gets his favourite pictures, the ones he loved the most, just because she thinks they are *pretty* but is too thick to appreciate their value."

"You had to stop her?"

"Well, she wasn't going to have them, and I wasn't going to take it. He should have loved me; he should have given them to me."

Her emotions were raw, she started to cry, but Clark didn't want her to stop. He tried to sound understanding, sympathetic even but he needed her to go on, complete the confession she had started.

"So, you confronted him?"

"We had a row, yes, and he fell over on one of my pictures. I was so angry I hit him. Only, I was holding a trowel at the time. I'd been using it to build a pizza oven in my garden you see. I didn't mean to kill him, but there he was."

"And what happened then?"

"I took him to his house, burnt his clothes because they were covered in my oil paint, and then I burnt my clothes because they were covered in blood."

"Why did you shoot him?"

"I don't know, mother, ..." she hesitated momentarily before composing herself and continuing. "When I was little mother always told me to clean up my mess, so I shot him on the bed, had a shower to clean myself up, got dressed and left."

Clark sensed she had just caught herself from saying something else and so latched onto the last word before her hesitation.

"And your mother helped you carry the body?"

"No, I did it all myself Inspector."

"We found a man's boot prints at the scene. The pattern appears similar to your husband's boots" He knew he hadn't had this confirmed yet but felt it was a solid enough deduction.

"I often wear my husband's boots when I'm working in the garden, His feet are so much bigger than mine it's easy to slip them on and off."

"So, are you telling me neither your husband or mother helped you dispose of the body?"

"No Inspector. He was heavy but I carried him all by myself; adrenaline I suppose. You hear of people being able to lift cars to free a loved one because of adrenaline, don't you? I guess that's what happened to me," adding defiantly, "and if you think otherwise you are going to have to prove it because I say she didn't"

Clark tried again, starting, "you said she didn't help carry him or do you mean she didn't, ..." but before he could complete his question, she interrupted him.

"Don't try and trick me Inspector. I confess to killing my stepfather, and I did it all alone."

"But it was an accident," suggested Clark, "an argument about a couple of paintings."

"That's right, an accident."

Clark considered for a moment. Could he get her to admit her mother had been her accomplice? Probably not. He decided to discuss the pictures with her, just to see her reaction.

"You know the paintings are fake?"

"Are they? Well, I suppose I should have let her have them then; she would have been happy enough. Bastard. Isn't that just typical of Donald; all flash and no substance."

"Two things are still bothering me," said Clark, "the wine?"

"Simple, I took some wine so I could get really, really, drunk."

"And why you were building a barbecue at all on such a hot day."

"That's easy Inspector, I just wanted to get it all done before our housewarming next week. We were going to have a party, invite everyone who couldn't come last year because of the Covid restrictions. Colin had been doing it, but what with work, and this and that, he keeps putting it off. So, I thought I'd just do it myself. Inspector, it isn't murder is it, if I say he attacked me first and I was just defending myself, is it? It would be better, wouldn't it?"

"It may have been if you hadn't moved the body and tried to cover it up, but as it is, I doubt it would make much difference at sentencing. Not now anyway."

She sat considering this for a moment before finally saying, "Life then? Good, that's fair."

They sat there together in tired silence, like long distance runners at the end of their marathon. They weren't rivals any longer but fellow competitors There was no sense of triumph from the policemen at obtaining the confession, just equal exhausted relief from them all.

It was Sarah who broke the silence.

"Do you think he knew?"

"What?"

"That the pictures were just worthless forgeries?"

"Maybe," explained Clark, "he left them to May knowing that they were fake. He knew she liked them as pictures and wouldn't care whoever painted them, to her they would never be worthless because she loved them for themselves, and because he gave them to her, not for the name on the signature. He knew, however, if you found out they weren't authentic, that it would ruin them for you. He didn't want to hurt you that way, because he did actually care about you."

"No, I can't let myself believe that." said Sarah, "why can't you just let me hate him.? If I don't hate him I won't be able to live with my guilt."

"I suppose it doesn't matter really, and anyway, I guess we'll never know."

It was late in the evening by the time Sarah's confession had been typed and finalised.

One of the first lessons every new detective has to learn is, you don't solve every case, it was a lesson Luca had yet to learn; for the good ones like Clark, even after years in the job, a part-solved case still chafes.

Outside the interview room Luca asked Clark "How are we going to be able to prove her mother helped her?"

"Well, somebody helped her, but honestly Luca," explained Clark, "I don't think we are. Sometimes in this job you have to take what you can get I'm afraid."

"So, her mother just gets away with it even though we all know she did it?"

"It's not what you know, it's about what the evidence you can present is actually worth in a court of law."

"But we know she has lied, time and again, we can prove that."

"True, but that doesn't prove she did anything. We need more, maybe only one thing more, but something linking her directly to the murder, and frankly, we've not got it."

"But there is no way Sarah could have carried Donald's body up the stairs without help. she helped cover it up and as accessory and we could charge her."

"There is this thing called reasonable doubt. Sarah says she did and it will be impossible to prove she didn't, and then show it was her mother that helped here and not say her husband, or someone else. We still need something irrefutable and at the moment we just don't have it."

"So, are we going to give up?"

"Where I'm going Constable, is I'm going to bed, and I suggest you do the same. You've done some extremely good work this week, just type up the paperwork for now. We've got Sarah today and we can always take another look at her mother in the morning, or next week. She'll still be there, and so will we."

"It just doesn't feel right."

"And I'd be disappointed if it did. We'll pick it up again tomorrow, and speak to her husband, but for now let's just call it a night. Okay?"

At the door, just as he was leaving, the desk Sergeant Ronnie Tutt stopped Clark.

"Inspector wait up a minute, I've still got the file you asked for."

"I'm sorry Ronnie," said Clark, "what with this murder case, I've forgotten what file I asked for?"

"You know, some old traffic report."

"Oh yeah, thanks Ronnie. I'm off home, I'll take it with me."

When he got home to his apartment Ella wasn't there waiting for him. He had forgotten he'd left her with June and was supposed to have collected her in the afternoon. Maybe he should call and apologise. There was a missed message on his phone, it read "If you ever want to see your dog again ring this number." He looked at the clock; nearly one in the morning, June would have to wait until tomorrow, no point waking her up now and getting into trouble twice. He'd pop round and apologise, coming to think of it he'd take some things round and cook her one of his famous breakfasts, he'd like to spend Sunday morning with her. Lately he'd been thinking about it more and more; maybe it was all these messed up families he spent his life investigating, lying and murdering one another, he needed someone like June, someone he had faith in, a person he could just trust.

Although he was tired Clark's mind was still going over and over the details. He poured himself a scotch and opened the file; it was a coroner's report on an old traffic incident from nearly eight years ago. An inquest had been held and returned a verdict of accidental death. Clark read it through slowly noting the main points. The accident happened on the way down the hill while going home from a skiing trip to Mt Hotham. It was a clear day but the road was icy. No other car had been involved. Marks on the road suggested the car had been travelling at speed and had lost control. The most probable cause was something major had failed at the front of the car, the suspension and steering were both implicated, although it was also possible it had been something wrong with the brakes. It was hard for the investigators to tell from the mangled wreckage wrapped around a tree.

Clark knew the route well and had attended a few accidents on the same stretch over the years. It was not uncommon for drivers to go off there, the road was particularly twisty; a treacherous stretch at the best of times, without winter ice adding to the dangers. A few years ago, he had almost come off the road himself driving at night when a deer had jumped out in front of him. He was sure for any coroner, accidental death, was an easy enough conclusion to come to. The thing about the report which bothered him however, was not that the driver Mr Sam Waters had killed himself, but the fact in doing so, he had also killed the only passenger in the car travelling with him, a young boy by the name of Angus McKay.

The freak accident had simultaneously killed both Emma McKay's then husband and the boy who would have become her stepson. If he had been feeling particularly charitable, the incident, he could have speculated, had perhaps even thrown the widow Emma Walters and Donald McKay closer together in their shared moment of grief. Given recent events however, he viewed the accident in a more sinister light.

He read through the file again looking for the details of the police crash scene examination report, but it wasn't there. Neither were any statements from the other family members explaining why the two had been in the car together in the first place. A slightly strange omission from the file, but not unheard of. There should be a transcript of the coroner's inquest somewhere. Maybe he would get Ronnie to dig it up from records. To Clark's way of thinking it all sounded like one coincidence too many, and as Clark had repeatedly learnt during his time in the police; a detective needed a healthy disrespect of coincidences.

And so, he went to bed, with the somewhat disquieting feeling Emma McKay had not gotten away with just one murder, but three.

All things considered; it had been an unsatisfying day. Hopefully tomorrow would be better.

For the past year successive lockdowns and changes to the states Covid regulations had not only damaged secular businesses; the eight o'clock eucharist at Holy Trinity had been particularly poorly attended. The dean did not blame anyone, it was just one of those things, something else to be grappled with in the quest for a new Covid normal. As he sat at his desk in the vestry, between services, the dean was worried, but the dean always was; worrying was in his job description. He was worried about the inadequate vaccination rates of his largely elderly congregation, he was worried that the wooden bell tower erected in 1983 to temporarily house the beautiful peal of eight Rudhall bells required more money to be spent on its maintenance than the diocese could currently afford, he was worried that the director of music had called to say that he was sick and wouldn't therefore be able to play the organ for the sung morning service at ten o'clock, and today he was particularly worried about Colin Roberts whose wife had recently been arrested.

Well, at least one of his problems should be easy enough to be solved. The dean picked up the phone and dialled. He heard the phone ring once, twice, three times, before it was answered.

"Morning Clark, it's Nick here, I'm sorry about the short notice but I was wondering if you were coming to mass this morning."

The organ at Holy Trinity is the fourth to be housed at the Cathedral. Built by famous organ makers Henry Willis & Sons in 1922 it is not the firm's magnum opus, that currently resides in Westminster Cathedral, nor is it the largest church organ in Australia, but its pipework and windchests make it tonally one of the finest and most widely respected. With its three keyboards, pedals and multiple rows of stops, it is not an instrument for the faint hearted, and not one that Clark ever turned down an opportunity to play.

Generally, Clark didn't attend the 10 o'clock service but when the dean phones it's very difficult to say no, even if your personal preferred worship was evensong, a service that not only makes you feel virtuous but one where you can go for a beer on the way home without the feeling that by doing so you have just undone any spiritual good you may have otherwise accrued.

Some mornings when the sun shines on its Warby granite façade Holy Trinity Cathedral radiates with a warm red luminosity. On those days, if you are lucky enough to be inside, the stained-glass glows and the simple red and black brick interior shines in universal welcome; which is of course exactly the point. The service had gone well, Clark had not pulled out all the stops, either literally or metaphorically, but any deficiencies in his playing had been sufficiently and adequately disguised by the choir so the congregation had hardly noticed, and the few whose musical ear was good enough to spot his occasional errors were far too polite to comment anyway. Clark had fun, while the dean had one less thing to worry about.

A beer may have been off the table, but morning tea wasn't, and Clark joined the dean, Sally Kendall, the diocesan registrar, and a small group of worshipers for the only post service brewed beverage on offer. It was not normally Clark's modus operandi to talk business with Sally and the Dean but today he decided to break that practice.

"Interesting service Nick," began Clark. The dean liked to be called simply Nick, without any title, while paradoxically insisting that one always be used when addressing the bishop.

"You liked my sermon on Matthew 19:24?"

"That's not what I meant," replied Clark, hoping at once that he hadn't sounded blunt and adding, "it was an interesting take on the text of course, I've always thought of that passage as a sort of idiom, you know kind of like saying *'you can't take it with you,'* but actually," he continued, eager to get the discussion away from the sermon, which had all been a bit scholarly for Clark's taste, "I was talking about your prayers this morning."

"Anything in particular?" asked the Dean, who obviously had noted Clark's original response, but was happy enough to let it go.

"You prayed for those affected by the terrible events this week. Were you referring to the murder of Donald McKay?"

"I was actually, horrible business I understand."

"Do you know the McKay's then?"

"Not really, they aren't church people, but I know his son-in-law Colin Roberts a little."

"And, if you don't mind me asking, how do you know him?"

"It's nothing secret Clark, not through the confessional. The diocese does some business through his firm, he's a solicitor you know."

Clark was just starting to regret he had brought it up, and hoping that they weren't going to ask him anything about the case when Sally joined in the discussion.

"I saw him on Tuesday actually."

"Donald McKay?"

"No Colin, I had a meeting with him at Saint John's about their registration paperwork."

"Saint John's the retirement home in town?"

"Nursing home," corrected Sally. "it took most of the day in the end. Good job he doesn't charge us his full rate."

"When you say most of the day?"

"The meeting lasted to almost three. We got through it all though, so it should be okay now. I think the Bishop is glad he'll never have to sit through another meeting about the place too."

"So, the Bishop was there as well, was he?"

"Oh yes, I really don't know why he wasted his day on it all though."

Reynold's 1st Rule of Detection was that innocent people have the worst alibis, because they don't need them, so you should always arrest the person with the best alibi. However, when the alibi is provided by both the diocesan registrar and the Bishop of Wangaratta, it was a rule he was willing to make an exception to.

The empty desks of the Wangaratta Police Station incident room resembled a scene from a ghost town. For Clark the case was not yet completed, but an arrest had been made, and without further information there was little left to do except tidy up.

Teddy sat at an abandoned desk listening as Clark and Alice gave him their summary.

"Clark, can you explain to me why Sarah Robert's confession doesn't put an end to it all?"

"I still think that his wife, Emma, is involved sir."

"I know you do but as far as I can see you haven't got any proof."

"Yet. Give me a few days more."

"And what's going to be different in a few days' time?"

It was a good question and Clark looked at the notes summarised on the white board while considering his reply.

"We've still got some video footage from town to go through."

"What will that achieve?"

"Well, if she appears in the morning we may know more about her true movements."

"But the best scenario there is you is spending a lot of time showing she is innocent, and her absence doesn't prove her guilt anyway, does it?"

Clark reconsidered. "At least let's look at all the timelines again."

"You can show me, Clark, but it had better be good. We had a second post office job over the weekend, and I'd like to use you on that, and I've had a request for Alice to help on another case that will mean her going a short secondment as well."

"Okay, This is Alice's timeline for Donald's last day."

Alice took up the story. As she spoke, she pointed to successive markers on her colour coded timeline. "Donald McKay had a late breakfast and left for work, driving past the SunniSleep Motel on his way into town, at 9:15, four minutes behind his wife Emma.

He arrived at his office just in time for a 9:30 appointment with his bank. That was scheduled to take half an hour but according to his PA Sandra it only went to about quarter to ten. Afterwards he had a brief Zoom meeting scheduled but due to internet problems ended up cancelling. Sandra estimates he left the office somewhere between half ten and eleven." She paused her narrative taking a drink from a water bottle before going on. "After that we don't know what he did for about half an hour, but he reappears at the Railway Café where he signed into on their Covid register at 11:36 and had Nachos. While there he made his last phone call to Luke Isleworth at 12:03 lasting about six minutes. Shortly after the call from the café, he paid for lunch using his credit card. That gets us to about 12.09 although the receipt is timed at 12:14, we think the clock on the till is actually wrong, but it's only a couple of minutes so probably not significant. Either way the waitress clearly remembers seeing him because he was apparently quite loud on the phone and rude to her when paying. Significantly, he didn't have coffee there, leaving presumably to see his stepdaughter and have a coffee with her instead, although like I said he didn't phone her to tell her he was coming round, which is a bit odd. There is one more time to look at, he was signed into the Arts Centre café at 1:55 by his wife. Interestingly, nobody remembers seeing him there, and she paid. We suspect that by that time he was already dead and she was just trying to establish her alibi.”

“So,” clarified Teddy, “killed between twelve and about two.”

“That seems to fit sir,”

“What does the doc say?”

“Not a lot. Apparently, there are too many unknown variables; it was a hot day and he was found in an air-conditioned room without clothes on. As we don’t know how long he had been undressed for, or when he was moved, she can’t say. The extremes of her modelling say time of death wouldn’t have been earlier than ten, and no later than four.”

“Not very helpful then.”

“Not really, but I’ve got a couple of other times to add in as well. A gun shot was heard at Willow Cottage about two, so his body had been transferred out there by then. We think it is likely that’s why she was at the café at two.”

“So Emma McKay’s accomplice could give her a 2 o’clock alibi?”

“That’s the theory.”

Teddy Edwards pointed to the whiteboard’s multicoloured timeline. “What’s this green stuff marked Frank?”

“That,” explained Clark pointed at the dotted part of the green timeline, “is our old friend Francis Young. Emma asked him to give her an alibi for the rest of the afternoon but he hasn’t. Here,” he added moving onto a solid part of the green line, “is when Frank and Emma McKay met with her divorce lawyer.”

“And you think that’s another red herring.”

"That's right. Why pay to see a divorce lawyer if you don't need a divorce?"

"Because you don't know your husband is dead."

"Or," suggested Clark, "because you want us to think you didn't know he was dead? I mean, who actually phones a divorce lawyer and demands a same afternoon emergency face to face divorce meeting?"

"But again, suspicious behaviour doesn't prove anything."

"But you can see that either way, while the meeting itself is an alibi at 4:00pm, we can't use it to assume she didn't know he was dead by then. What we do know is that after that meeting, at around five, she didn't go straight home because she wasn't filmed on her way home until 6:23pm. My guess is she went to her daughter's house on her way to see if everything had gone to plan first. Incidentally she didn't phone the police station until 7:14pm. That gave her a good half hour at home to double check everything before calling us."

"What about the son-in-law Colin Roberts in all this?"

"Now, you'll like this, he really does have a cast iron alibi."

Through years of working together Teddy was well aware of Reynold's *Rule of Alibis* and could hardly help himself asking.

"What do mean cast iron?"

"The Bishop of Wangaratta among others."

"Okay, and don't get me wrong, you and Alice have done a good job, but I don't see anything here other than you being able to show that his wife had more than enough time which we can't account for. We've made an arrest, so let's call this one a win and get on with other things."

"Just give me a couple of days to see if we can track her movements down a bit better."

"I'm sorry Clark, if it wasn't for this bloody armed robbery, I'd give them to you but I'm calling this one."

"If we get something else?"

"Don't think it doesn't annoy me too Clark. If your gut says that she did it, I believe you, and if someone comes forward, we can always have another look then, but while we're so thin on the ground I think it's time to move on."

Although a superintendent, Teddy rarely gave a direct order, but Clark knew him well enough to recognise the force carried by one of his suggestions; Clark nodded his acknowledgement.

"Speaking of thin on the ground, have you decided what you're going to do with Luca Bastoni yet?"

"He's yours for six months if you want him."

Here and there, everywhere
Scenes that we once knew
And they all just recall
Memories of you
Eubie Blake and Andy Razaf

A string of black cars pulled up outside the Wangaratta funeral home. For one of the occupants, the short journey from the farm, which for over a hundred years had been called Willow Cottage, would be his last. Inside the front vehicle, the body of the man who had been Donald McKay lay inside an elegant box. The funeral arrangements were not what he would have wanted, but his desires were no longer being considered.

Mrs Emma McKay emerged from the second car. She was dressed, as was traditional, in widow's black; and she wore it well. At her side came her sister, looking like a bridesmaid trying hard to not upstage the star of the show, and nobody watching could have been mistaken Emma McKay was the star; the corpse of her recently deceased husband reduced to little more than a stage prop for her sham grief.

The celebrant greeted her and guided her inside where a small gathering had assembled; they stood around awkwardly trying to make small talk. The coffin followed carried by six members of the funeral home's staff. That Donald McKay did not have sufficient friends to carry his casket said more about him than any eulogy could.

Behind Emma McKay and the immediate family sat a small knot of mourners. Clark recognised Donald McKay's assistant Sandra and Frank Young. The rest Clark supposed were friends and business contacts. Clark and Alice edged over to sit near Tony Boor. At the back of the chapel stood a heavily set man with an unkempt beard, long hair and sunglasses with the same confident yet cumbersome pose usually adopted by night club bouncers. Under his suit he wore a black shirt open at the collar one button further than strictly appropriate. Clark wondered if this was Stevie Dunn, and if it was why he would have come.

The most noticeable absentee was his stepdaughter, Sarah Roberts. She had wanted to go, and Inspector Clark Reynolds had tried to make the suitable arrangements, but her mother had told her it would be for the best, under the circumstances, if she didn't make a personal appearance. The inspector and his sergeant attended instead, bringing a wreath with them on her behalf.

The ceremony in no way reflected Donald McKay as a person, how could it, the celebrant had never met him. She did her best, but her best, under these restrictions, was not very good. His first wife was not mentioned, nor was his son, Angus, or daughter May Richardson. His relationship with the woman who, in retrospect, could have been considered as his truest love, his sister-in-law Jeanie Jones was similarly, and discretely, not revealed. There was no celebration of his life or of his unique individuality. Instead, the celebrant trotted out a list of usual platitudes: he was a devoted husband, he had a favourite song, was a prominent and a respected member of the community who will be widely missed by all who knew him. It all could have been equally applicable to anyone, items taken from a shallow menu of routine grief. And yet Donald, the man, had loved, experienced the joy of a son, and the grief of his loss; he had a daughter he had hardly known, but regretted his relationship with her had not been more. All he had done, felt, achieved; was it fair to his memory that it be reduced to this, a standardised service delivered by a stranger? Was this, really, all he merited? Was this hollow farce all his life was worth?

The question of what a life is worth had been much discussed lately, Covid-19 business grants and the cost to the economy from the successive lockdowns aimed at saving as many lives as possible had seen to that. There were those that argued that anything that harmed their business, however well intentioned, was an intolerable imposition. Clark had seen enough death to know that life could never be purchased. It was therefore, by any definition priceless, to be cherished, and after one's life was over, its uniqueness deserved to be remembered with respectful dignity.

Clark, like the celebrant, had never met Donald McKay, and yet he felt he knew something of the man. He had spoken to those who knew him best, and some who knew the worst of him. He had taken the trouble to learn both his story and his measure. To Clark, Donald McKay was a person, and Donald deserved better than this, anyone did.

And if Clark hadn't known anything about Donald McKay, and like the celebrant not bothered to find anything out either, he would have used the traditional language; "man that is born of a woman hath but a short time to live, and is full of misery", and committed, "his body to the ground; earth to earth, ashes to ashes, dust to dust," so that at the very least Donald would have been treated to some parting poetry. Instead, all Clark had heard was a pile of inconsequential contrived rubbish about what football team Donald barracked for, as if that explained any part of his role in the universe or gave succour to his dearly beloved. The truth was, for all his beautiful old farmhouse, filled with fine paintings and antiques, new cars and other signs of worldly wealth, he had brought nothing into this world, and would carry nothing out. Perhaps, thought Clark, it would have been better in the end to just say so.

Clark's dark mood was not enhanced by his conviction Emma McKay was complicit in the murder. He had not yet completely resigned himself to the fact she had walked free, leaving her daughter to carry the costs, while she, as a free woman, got on with her life. It was an unsettling feeling compounded by his instinct it was not the first murder she had walked away from with impunity. Clark believed in the system; in crime, punishment and the scales of justice. In Clark's morality actions should have consequences, and a murder should be followed by a reckoning, and yet he failed to see how he could ever bring this about. Not without the step-daughter's cooperation anyway. It did not sit well with him.

Clark looked over the assembled congregation towards Emma McKay. She looked back at him as if acknowledging her understanding of his frustrations. Her performance as the grieving widow was impeccable. Clark decided he was not going to stay and sit through the remainder of it. He would not give her the satisfaction. He had not been able to arrest her as Donald McKay's murderer but he owed the man that much at least. He left.

As the door slowly closed behind him, Clark heard the remaining mourners begin to sing the old hymn, *Guide Me O Thou Great Redeemer*. It was somehow fitting, to Clark's musical ear, so many of the congregation were singing in the wrong key.

Bring out a thousand policemen, bring 'em around today
To lock me down in the dungeon cell, and throw that key away

Hugo Cannon and Bill Dooley

Sunday breakfast was a meal June took seriously. Eggs Florentine on fresh sourdough, and a side serve of mushrooms. All eaten while tackling the Border Informer's famous weekend trivia quiz. There were thirty questions and Clark and June decided to split the quiz in half and see which of them could get the most right. Clark knew he'd have to be pretty lucky to beat June but somehow didn't mind, it was a weekly drubbing he was happy to accept.

"Question 14," asked Clark taking another mouthful, "which movie held the record for the highest grossing box office receipts in Australia before Titanic?"

June thought for a moment, "I don't know, when was Titanic released, late 1990's?"

"That," encouraged Clark, "sounds about right."

"Given it's a local paper, I'm going to guess an Australian film from the 1980's, let's say, Crocodile Dundee."

"Correct again. Okay Question 15, ..." He stopped in mid-sentence.

"Clark, what's the matter? Clark?"

"Sorry, it was just thinking about films and cameras. It just made me think of the case."

June didn't have to ask which case was still troubling him.

"Give me a minute."

Clark took his phone out of his pocket and dialled.

"Alice? Sorry to do this to you at home but you know your motel camera footage from the McKay case."

"Yeah, but I've not actually looked at it all, Luca did."

"Is he working today?"

"Yes but, because last week he didn't get his day off, I told him he could come in late today."

"Can you get him to come into the station in ten minutes and show it to me anyway?"

"Are we still on the McKay case then?"

"Of course."

He hung up.

"It's okay," June told him. "Just go or it will be bugging you all day. I know what you're like."

"Are you sure?"

"You go. Ella and I will be fine."

Sitting in the car Clark found himself thinking, June was right, the drive into the station from her house wasn't really any further than from his flat. She was always right about these things. Maybe it was time he moved in; time to make an honest woman of her. If she hadn't said, when they first started to go out, she never wanted to get married, he may have asked her years ago. Clark wondered if he should have taken her at her word. He wasn't one for deep and meaningful discussions but he would have to give it some serious thought.

As Luca cued the video footage on his computer, Clark asked him, "Luca, tell me about Sam Winters."

"What do you want to know?"

"Well," said Clark, "start with what he did for a living."

"Sam had a bike shop," Luca told him, before elaborating, "motorbikes not pushbikes."

"Where was that?"

"I don't know, South Melbourne somewhere. Great bikes though," Luca reminisced, "I remember going there once and seeing all these one-off custom Harley Davidsons, you know, choppers, like in *Easy Rider*."

"The sort of thing bikies ride?"

"I suppose so, they would have to be rich bikies though; those things aren't cheap."

"And how did your dad know him then?"

"Through bikes. My dad used to race a bit when he was younger, not very well actually, he fell off a few times more than is good for you. He still walks with a limp."

"So, I bet you know a great mechanic?"

"Not really but my dad would. I could ask him for you if your car needs a tune-up."

"It's alright, Constable, I'm not looking to pimp-my-ute; and I suppose that means Mrs McKay would know the odd mechanic or two herself."

"I expect so. What's this about sir?"

"I was just thinking about Sam Winter's crash and the mysterious car failure."

"Didn't Emma McKay say it was an accident?"

"She would, wouldn't she, but it's not often you have a cars suspension collapse these days, not without someone playing with it. Anyway," continued Clark, "it was a long time ago and we aren't likely to get anywhere with it now. Is this motel video ready yet?"

"Just about. What are we looking for sir?"

"Well Constable, you said you saw Mrs McKay drive past twice, once after nine in the morning on her way into town, and again just before half past six in the evening on her way home. Did she also drive past in the middle of the day?"

"Definitely not sir, I watched for her car very carefully."

"And what time," asked Clark, "did Sarah drive out there with Mr McKay's body in the boot of her car?"

"I've no idea, I wasn't looking for her. What car does she drive?"

Clark couldn't remember. The supposedly stolen car had never been recovered. They both looked at Alice.

"I don't know." Alice thought for a moment, "why not try looking for a little red and white hatchback."

"Of course," said Luca, "but this will take a while."

"Let's figure it out then," encouraged Clark. "We can distil Alice's timeline down to a couple of key pieces of information. To start with we can be sure he was alive as 12:03 because he made a phone call to Luke Isleworth. Then, at about two o'clock his wife was already trying to establish her alibi, so we can assume he was dead by then."

"Wasn't the gun shot heard at two as well?"

"So, if it takes 10 or fifteen minutes to drive between Wangaratta and the house, we should be concentrating on his body being taken out there sometime between ten past twelve and ten to two."

Luca slid the scroll marker on his computer to about the middle of the film and set play to high speed. As they watched the small computer screen cars and trucks flashed past in an indistinguishable blur."

"Okay Luca," admitted Clark, "we can't see anything at this speed you're going to have to slow it down."

Luca adjusted the controls. Now the vehicles were still moving unnaturally quickly but could almost be identified. Soon one appeared large enough to show up clearly, a white delivery van hurtling past only to return almost immediately in the other direction."

"Stop it there," Clark ordered, "that's the wine delivery, we've gone too far."

A few more cars flashed past as Luca pressed the pause key. Luca checked the time stamp, 2:11: his inspector was right.

"Now," instructed Clark. "Just go back slowly from here."

Leisurely this time the cars went by, reversing across the screen, those from Wangaratta bunched into small groups by the roadworks just down the road from the motel. Then a red and white one drove into view. A small European hatchback on its way out of town travelling towards Willow Cottage, just like the one Pete King had told them he had seen.

Luca pressed pause and enlarged the image to full screen size. There, behind the steering wheel, and clear to see, was Sarah Roberts. It was also possible to see another person was sitting next to her, but because she was on the far side of the street from the camera position, her face was hidden.

"Can we get a better view of the passenger?" asked Clark.

"I'll try."

Luca clicked back the film, inching one frame at a time until the two figures in the car were clearly separated. He tried zooming in the image again. This time both figures were identifiable, Sarah Roberts driving, while seated next to her it was clearly possible to make out the face of her husband Colin. The pictures didn't show a third person was also in the car, but they had already satisfied themselves Donald McKay was there too, dead and in the boot.

When Luca had first been assigned to the unit, he had started off believing, somehow, he was better than the other two, and working with them was just a stepping stone to higher things. Now he was starting to see his career differently. Alice's example had showed Luca that it was not about him, his value was as part of a team, and while he still believed that the team was stronger with him than without, he understood he was stronger as part of the team. His reward would not come through his status or promotion but by serving his community.

The three police officers looked at each other and then back to the screen. It had been a difficult few days. As a team, the three all realised the significance of Colin Robert's image at the same time. The two more experienced officers left it to the young constable to voice their collective feelings with one word.

"Gotcha!"

Alice looked at Clark and was about to say something, but he already had his phone in his hand and was dialling.

"Sally, it's Clark… You remember that chat the other day about some meeting you had with Colin Roberts and the Bishop… Yes, the nursing home meeting…Well was Colin Roberts at the meeting all day? … He wasn't… What time was that… So, you can't vouch for him after about 12? … No that's alright I must have misunderstood what you said that's all… I just assumed if the meeting lasted all day, he would have been there the whole time… No, it's my fault… Sorry, I can't really say anything more now… I'll see you later? … "

After he had hung up Alice caught his eye, "It's another win for Reynold's 1st Rule of Detection after all then. Let's go and arrest the guy with the alibi."

"I still don't believe it, Colin and Sarah. They are such nice people," interjected Luca, "and out of curiosity, where does Emma McKay fit into all this now?"

"Let's go and find out," stated Clark.

"But you still believe she's guilty and may still get away with it?"

"Ultimately Constable, I believe we all go and meet our maker, and on that day, the worth of every man is calculated; in front of our final judge nobody gets away with anything. Every policeman has to learn to accept that, because the ones who can't and end up obsessing over every single missed conviction, well, that's what eats them up inside."

"I'm not sure I understand sir."

"Hopefully one day you will, until then we'd better go and arrest Colin Roberts and see what he has to say for himself."

"And, if he doesn't implicate Emma McKay just accept we have two out of the three?"

"At some point you must ask yourself, 'have I done my best?'."

"And if you have," suggested Luca, "then in the words of Brutus '*We must take the current when it serves*'?"

"Well, I was thinking more about the singer Meatloaf, but yes, now you're getting it detective. Welcome to C.I.D."

In the car on the way to arrest Colin Roberts, Clark asked himself if he really meant that, he would ever be happy with two out of three. He knew that he wouldn't, and at some point in the future he would have to see what he could do about Emma McKay. If nothing else, is it really justice for Donald and his son Angus if the case closed as it was, but maybe that was just him. Luca was a good young officer, as long as two out of three was enough to get the best out of him at this stage in his career, he'd go along with it just a little while longer, and you never know, Colin might be an easier nut to crack than his mother-in-law.

Never saw the sun shining so bright
Never saw things going so right
Noticing the days hurrying by
When you're in love, my how they fly

Irving Berlin

As Clark carried the last box inside, past the doorbell that had already been relabelled, through the hallway stripped of his old jazz memorabilia, and on into the front room. Luca was already unpacking.

"That's it?"

"I think so," said Luca handing his inspector a bottle in a brown paper bag as a way of thanks. "Something for all your help."

Clark took it without protest. He peeked inside the bag, it was a single malt, a fair exchange for his labours. He offered Luca a "you're welcome. Just don't move again, I've shifted more than enough boxes for a while," comment as an acknowledgement, before adding, "yes, this place should suit you. It was a pretty good flat for me for a few years."

"Do you want a drink or anything before you go?"

"I'd better not. I've left Ella in the car and June will be wondering where I've got to."

Two minutes later, after shutting his old front door for the last time Clark was climbing into his ute. His dog Ella, strapped onto the rear seat, looked up as he entered.

"Come on girl, let's get going and find your mum."

As he pulled out, Ella Fitzgerald's voice sang out from the car radio.

Bluebirds singing a song
Nothing but blue skies from now on

THE END

If you have enjoyed this book, look out for the next instalment as Inspector Reynolds faces his biggest case yet in *Speak Not Of Hope,* out mid-2026.

The following is brief contextual note about each of the song extracts used throughout this work including some notable recordings that the reader may enjoy.

To the best of the author's knowledge, all song extracts referenced in this book were first published in the USA prior to 1929 and/or it is more than seventy years since the author's death, making them therefore, in the public domain, and they have been used without the intention of breaching copyright.

St. James Infirmary Blues

I went down to the Infirmary,
Saw my baby there,
Stretched out on a long white table,
So cold, so sweet, so fair.
Don Redman and Joe Primrose

Sheet music for this song was first published in 1925 as the "*Gambler's Blues*" credited to Carl Moore and Phil Baxter but it is now generally known as "*St. James Infirmary Blues*" following Louis Armstrong's renaming and reworking the song on his 1928 recording.

Armstrong's version credits Don Redman as composer, while later releases also co- credit "Joe Primrose", (a pseudonym used by producer Irving Mills.)

The Big Butter and Egg Man

She wants somebody, who's workin' all day
So she's got money, when she wants to play
Venable and Armstrong

Written in 1926 by Percy Venable and originally recorded in the same year by Louis Armstrong and His Hot Five it is now normally co-credited to Venable and Armstong.

Oh, Lady Be Good!

Oh, please have some pity
I'm all alone in this big city
I tell you I'm just a lonesome babe in the wood
So lady, be good to me
George and Ira Gershwin

Written in 1924 by George and Ira Gershwin it first appeared in the Broadway musical of the same name starring Fred and Adele Astaire.

The song was also performed in the unconnected 1941 film of the same name *"Lady Be Good."*

It has been recorded by numerous artists since 1925 and became a hit in 1947 for Ella Fitzgerald.

Mack the Knife

Though the shark's teeth may be lethal
Still you see them white and red
But you won't see Mackie's flick knife
Cause he slashed you and you're dead
Kurt Weill and Bertolt Brecht

First published as *"Die Moritat von Mackie Messer"* by Kurt Weill with lyrics by Bertolt Brecht for their 1928 music drama *"The Threepenny Opera"* (German, *"Die Dreigroschenoper."*)

It has been recorded many times by the likes of Louis Armstrong, Bobby Darin, Ella Fitzgerald and Frank Sinatra and is most commonly sung using the translated lyrics of Marc Blitzstein.

Who'll Take My Place When I'm Gone

Everything must have an end
So the poets say
Our romance like all the rest
Will end some sorry day
Raymond Klages and Billy Fazioli.

Published by Broadway Music Corporation in 1922, and first recorded in the same year by the Moulin Rouge Orchestra.

I'll Be Glad When You're Dead a.k.a.
You Rascal You

When you're dead and in your grave
No more women, who you crave
I'll be glad when you're dead, you rascal, you!

Sam Theard

Written by Sam Theard in 1929 and titled *"I'll Be Glad When You're Dead"* it quickly achieved the status of jazz standard as *"You Rascal You"* with hit versions by The Mills Brothers (1932), Red Nichols & His Five Pennies (1931), Cab Calloway (1931) and Louis Armstrong (1931)

How come you do me like you do ?

Treat me right or else just let me be
'Cause I can beat you doing what you're doing to me
How come you do me like you do do do?

Gene Austin and Roy Bergere

Written by Gene Austin and Roy Bergere in 1924, (better known as a vaudeville comedy duo.) It has been repeatedly covered by many artists including, Louis Armstrong, Lead Belly, Cab Calloway, Bing Crosby, Duke Ellington, Benny Goodman, Coleman Hawkins and Julie London.

Sinner Man

Oh, Sinnerman, where you gonna run to?
Sinnerman, where you gonna run to?
Where you gonna run to?
All along dem day
Les Baxter and Will Holt

The writing credit on the earliest recording of the song "*Sinner Man*" is by Les Baxter and folk singer Will Holt although it is clearly derived from an old spiritual "*No Hiding Place Down Here*", as recorded in 1928 by the Old South Quartette.

"*Sinnerman*" (spelled as one word) is one of Nina Simone's most famous songs and has also recorded by reggae artists Peter Tosh and Bunny Wailer.

In 2020, Australian duo Vika and Linda Ball covered the song on their Covid-19 pandemic lockdown album, *Sunday (The Gospel According to Iso)*.

Down Hearted Blues

Trouble, trouble
I've had it all my days
It seems like trouble
Going to follow me to my grave
Lovie Austin and Alberta Hunter

Recorded in 1922 and credited to Lovie Austin and Alberta Turner (updated later to Alberta Hunter). It was soon covered in 1923 by Bessie Smith (who sold over 2 million copies.) Subsequently, it has become a jazz and blues standard.

Mean to Me

You're mean to me
Why must you be mean to me?
Gee, honey, it seems to me
You love to see me cryin'
Fred Ahlert and Roy Turk

First published in 1929, with hit versions that year by both Ruth Etting and by Helen Morgan. As an established standard it has been recorded multiple times by a who's who of jazz musicians.

There is a fabulous version by Ella Fitzgerald, accompanied by pianist Oscar Peterson on the 1975 album *Ella and Oscar*.

The Song Is Ended
(But the Melody Lingers On)
The moon descended
And I found with the break of dawn
You and the song had gone
But the melody lingers on
Irving Berlin

First published in 1927 by Irving Berlin *"The Song is Ended"* is perhaps most associated these days sung by Ella Fitzgerald from her 1958 award-winning, *"Ella Fitzgerald Sings the Irving Berlin Songbook."*

Ira Gershwin's 1937 *"They Can't Take That Away from Me"* references the song in the line *"the song is ended, but as the songwriter wrote, the melody lingers on. "*

Memories of You

Here and there, everywhere
Scenes that we once knew
And they all just recall
Memories of you
Eubie Blake and Andy Razaf

"Memories of You," was composed in 1930 by Eubie Blake and Andy Razaf and has been recorded by artists as diverse as Louis Armstrong, and Benny Goodman.

It should not be confused with the Beatles song *"Here, There and Everywhere"* from their 1966 album *"Revolver."*

Frankie and Johnny

Bring out a thousand policemen, bring 'em around
today
To lock me down in the dungeon cell, and throw that
key away
Hugo Cannon and Bill Dooley

In 1899 Bill Dooley composed *"Frankie Killed Allen"* shortly after the Frankie Baker murder case, when Baker shot his lover Allen 'Albert' Britt. The first published version of the music to *"Frankie and Johnny"* appeared in 1904, credited to Hughie 'Hugo' Cannon.

The song has also been recorded as *"Frankie and Johnnie"*, *"Frankie and Albert"* or just *"Frankie,"* with the writing credited for the alternate versions co-given to the assorted performers or sometimes as "traditional."

Blue Skies

Never saw the sun shining so bright
Never saw things going so right
Noticing the days hurrying by
When you're in love, my how they fly

Bluebirds singing a song
Nothing but blue skies from now on

Irving Berlin

Written by Irving Berlin as an additional tune included in the 1926 musical *"Betsy"* by Rodgers and Hart, *"Blue Skies"* became an instant stage hit with audiences demanding multiple encores at the premiere.

It came to international fame when Al Jolson performed it in the first talking movie *"The Jazz Singer."* (1927)

www.ingramcontent.com/pod-product-compliance
Lightning Source LLC
Chambersburg PA
CBHW051759050726
47598CB00006B/2347